"I'm Taking You Shopping," He Said. "For Whatever You Need For This Role."

"This role?" she echoed.

"As my lover, my girlfriend, my mistress, my woman. Which would you prefer?"

"No." She shook her head adamantly. "I won't do it. I would rather scrub floors."

"You came here tonight to ascertain your role as my employee." Suddenly his expression was decisive, his demeanour all brooking-no-argument business. "I do not need household help of any variety. I need you here, as my lover."

"Your *pretend* lover."

And when he closed down the space between them, she held her ground and held his gaze. "I have every confidence in you, Isabelle," he said evenly, but there was a hint of wicked in both voice and eyes as they drifted over her face. "I believe you will satisfy me in any role you take on, whether pretend or otherwise."

Dear Reader,

Do you remember when you first started reading romance? I was young—I don't recall exactly how young, but my mother used to order the *English Woman's Weekly*, which carried serialized Mills and Boon novels. Waiting for the next issue to see what happened next was torturous, and I was soon seeking and devouring the books.

Many of my favorites were set in London and the English countryside, as were many of my family's television favorites of the time: *Upstairs, Downstairs; The Forsyte Saga; The Avengers*. This firmly seeded in me a love of all things English. The accents, the manners, the stately homes, the countryside and cottages and hedgerows. My favorite movie list includes *Love, Actually; Notting Hill; Four Weddings and a Funeral* and *Pride and Prejudice*.

Setting one or more of my books in England was inevitable, and the stories of sisters Isabelle and Chessie Browne fit perfectly. My first visit to England was for *my* sister's wedding, you see, and I was lucky enough to return a couple of years ago and revisit some of my favorite spots—and find some new ones—in and around London. These added to a lifetime of beloved reading and viewing experiences to create the world of this book.

It is an extremely affluent world, one Isabelle has only experienced as a housekeeper to the wealthy, and even then she's seen nothing like the townhouse or the country estate belonging to Cristiano Verón. She is swept into a world of polo and personal shoppers and charity benefits, a fairy-tale world she believes fits no better than the couture clothes and designer shoes.

I hope you enjoy Isabelle's Cinderella transformation and that you will look out for Chessie's book, titled *Billionaire's Inconvenient Bride*, in January 2010.

Cheers,

Bronwyn

BRONWYN JAMESON

MAGNATE'S MAKE-BELIEVE MISTRESS

Silhouette®

Desire

Published by Silhouette Books

America's Publisher of Contemporary Romance

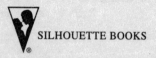

SILHOUETTE BOOKS

PLEASE RECYCLE
THIS PRODUCT IS RECYCLABLE

ISBN-13: 978-0-373-76955-1

Recycling programs
for this product may
not exist in your area.

MAGNATE'S MAKE-BELIEVE MISTRESS

Books by Bronwyn Jameson

Silhouette Desire

In Bed with the Boss's Daughter #1380
Addicted To Nick #1410
Zane: The Wild One #1452
Quade: The Irresistible One #1487
A Tempting Engagement #1571
Beyond Control #1596
Just a Taste #1645
*The Rugged Loner #1666
*The Rich Stranger #1680
*The Ruthless Groom #1691
The Bought-and-Paid-for Wife #1743
Back in Fortune's Bed #1777
Vows & a Vengeful Groom #1843
Tycoon's One-Night Revenge #1865
Magnate's Make-Believe Mistress #1955

*Princes of the Outback

BRONWYN JAMESON

spent much of her childhood with her head buried in a book. As a teenager, she discovered romance novels, and it was only a matter of time before she turned her love of reading them into a love of writing them. Bronwyn shares an idyllic piece of the Australian farming heartland with her husband and three sons, a thousand sheep, a dozen horses, assorted wildlife and one kelpie dog. She still chooses to spend her limited downtime with a good book. Bronwyn loves to hear from readers. Write to her at bronwyn@bronwynjameson.com or visit her Web site at www.bronwynjameson.com.

For the Maytoners; this pair of books
was blessed by your brainstorming.

One

"Steady, baby, there is no rush. We have all the time in the world." Cristiano Verón shifted his weight over Gisele's back, the touch of his hand on her neck as deeply soothing as his voice. Between his legs, she quivered with contained excitement as their pace eased to a smooth, rolling rhythm.

"Good girl," he murmured. Another slow caress from ear to shoulder echoed his praise. "Perfect."

Gisele was so responsive, so biddable, so willing to please. So unlike the other females in his life, although that cynical observation did not dampen his bone-deep pleasure of this moment nor dim his satisfied smile. The verdant scent of spring filled his nostrils. Glorious sunshine warmed his back and arms for the first time in weeks. And when he swung his polo stick, the smack of contact with the ball fired exhilaration through his body.

Not better than sex, but hitting the polo field—even stick-

and-balling alone—ranked second on Cristo's personal pleasure scale.

Lately there'd been too few opportunities for pleasure. He could not recall the last weekend that wasn't built around business or family obligations, or the last Sunday he'd spent at his Hertfordshire estate. And, *Dios,* he missed his stables, he missed his ponies, he missed the passion and the controlled aggression of this game.

With a light press of his thighs, Cristo guided the favourite of his ponies through a series of sure-footed turns. As always, she responded sweetly, answering every command without argument. If only that were true of—

The thought stopped dead. Cristo's eyes narrowed on the lone figure standing dead centre of his practice pitch. Not one of the females hell-bent on driving him loco, but a near relation.

Hugh Harrington, his sister's fiancé.

Resigned to the interruption Cristo swore softly but without heat. It wasn't that he disliked his future brother-in-law. Hugh had pursued Amanda with the same single-minded purpose he displayed on the polo pitch, and that steadfast attitude had earned Cristo's grudging approval. Now if Hugh were standing midfield in his polo kit, Cristo would have welcomed his arrival with unbridled delight. But no, the younger man wore business clothes and an expression of grim determination on his pretty-boy face.

Another wedding drama, Cristo predicted. The damned event had turned into a circus of mammoth dimensions, and since Cristo was writing the cheques, he also suffered through the daily crises reported by Amanda and their mother.

He reminded himself it would be over in less than a month. Amanda would lose the manic bride-to-be tic. Vivi would resume her pursuit of husband number five. Life would return to normal.

Just twenty-eight more days…

Easing Gisele to a halt, he greeted his unexpected visitor with a laconically raised brow. "I thought you were casting your eye over a property in Provence."

"Finished the appraisal, flew home last night," Hugh said. Straightening his shoulders, he drew a breath that puffed out his chest. "I'm sorry to intrude on your practice, and on a Sunday. I won't keep you long, but I have to speak with you."

"That sounds ominous. What is it this time?" Cristo asked mildly. "Roses refusing to bloom? Caterer resigned in a snit? Another bridesmaid turned up pregnant?"

Hugh's south-of-France tan blanched. "Not a bridesmaid," he muttered.

"Amanda?"

"No, another woman. I don't know who she is," Hugh said in an agitated rush. "Except she's Australian and she called while I was away and left this bloody message on my voice mail. She says she's pregnant."

Gisele threw her head, alerting Cristo that he'd unconsciously tightened his grip on the reins. He gentled the pony's skittishness with a hand on her neck, but his gaze remained fixed on the younger man's harried countenance. "Are you telling me this woman is expecting your child?"

"That is her claim, but it's absolute bollocks."

"You said you don't know who she is." Cristo spoke slowly, each word a clear bite of disbelief. His voice was no longer mild. "Are you saying you have never met?"

"How can I say that for sure? You know I was in Australia for almost a month earlier this year, preparing for the Hillier estate sale."

Hugh travelled widely and often as a representative of his family's auction house, but Cristo did specifically remember the trip because of his lovelorn sister's response to her fiancé's long absence. Amanda was a firm believer in the adage of misery loves company.

"I daresay I met hundreds of people," Hugh continued.

"Some of them women, no doubt."

"I didn't meet them in that way. I was pointing out that I *may* have met this woman, but I don't recall her by name. Since I asked Amanda to be my wife, I haven't looked at anyone else. Why would I risk everything that is my happiness?"

If not for his cynicism toward love and marriage, Cristo might have swallowed that ardently delivered speech. But he also subscribed to one of his stepfather's oft-quoted beliefs: *Where there's smoke, there is fire.* "Does anyone else know about this woman's claim?" he asked.

Hugh shook his head.

"You haven't told Amanda?"

"Are you serious? You know what state she is in with the wedding preparations."

Sadly, Cristo did.

"She deserves nothing less than a perfect day. What if this woman were to turn up here, on my doorstep, the day before the wedding?"

"What are you planning to do?" Cristo asked. "Pay her off?"

Hugh blinked in astonishment, as if he'd not considered that as an option. Cristo wondered if he'd considered any options. "I don't know what to do," he said, confirming that judgement. "I would have consulted Justin, but he's in New York patching up Harringtons' reputation. I couldn't lumber him with another problem on top of this last year, which is why I'm seeking your advice."

Cristo had no problem with that choice and acknowledged it with a single nod. On top of his wife's death, Hugh's elder brother was dealing with an internal scandal in the American office of his family's venerable firm. According to rumours, the fallout was not pretty.

"Why me?" Hugh shook his head with apparent bemusement. "She must have chosen me for a reason."

Cristo could think of several billion. "Did she mention money?" he asked.

"She didn't mention much at all. She said she'd been trying to reach me for the past week. She asked if I remembered her—even spelt her name out, as if that were significant. Then she came right out with 'I'm pregnant.'"

"She sounds like a woman who doesn't mince words."

"She sounded like a woman who was ticked off. What should I do, Cristo? I can't risk Amanda finding out, nor can I ignore this…this…" Hugh raked a hand through his hair and expelled a broken breath. "Maybe it's a misunderstanding. Or a case of mistaken identity. Maybe I should just call her."

"Do you have her number?"

Hugh produced a sheet of notepaper from his inside jacket pocket. For a second, Cristo watched it shake in his hand. Despite the holiday tan, he looked wan and rattled, and Cristo had to wonder at the cause. Perhaps the old love-'em-and-leave-'em Hugh Harrington—the one his brother Justin had been called on to rescue from numerous past scrapes—had come out to play on that lengthy business trip.

A world away from home, a few too many drinks, a beautiful temptress who didn't mince words…

Perhaps that explained his reluctance to confide in Amanda, or to return the woman's call. Perhaps he'd come here today acting the part of bewildered innocence, confident that Cristo would pay off the momentary blunder and make her go away. He knew that family was everything to Cristo, that he would do anything to ensure his sister's happiness.

"Are you going to call her?" Hugh asked.

"I have a trip to Australia scheduled for early in June. I can bring it forward." Cristo made the decision on the spot, forming a plan of action as he spoke. "It would be desirable to meet this woman in person and as soon as possible. To discover exactly what she wants."

"You'd do that for me?"

"No," he replied tersely. "I'll do that for Amanda."

Leaning down, he plucked the fluttering page from Hugh's hand. *Isabelle Browne,* he read. Then a telephone number and what looked like a business name. "At Your Service?" Eyes narrowed, he looked up sharply. "Is this an escort agency?"

"I have no idea. I wrote that down from her message. I gather it's a business name, but it means nothing to me." Hugh's head came up a notch. A look of alarm pinched his expression. "You don't believe me, do you?"

"I don't *dis*believe you, but I prefer to make up my own mind."

"By trying to find this Isabelle Browne?"

"I will find her," Cristo corrected in a lethally low voice. "And I will discover the truth behind her allegation before I walk my sister down the aisle. If it turns out you are lying, there will be no payout, no hiding the truth and no wedding."

"Everything I have said is the truth, Cristo, I swear."

"Then you have nothing to worry about, do you?"

Isabelle Browne had spent twenty-four hours convincing herself she had nothing to worry about. The man who'd booked her as his housekeeper for the next week was CEO and Chairman of a private aviation firm. Any one of Chisholm Air's high-flying clients could have recommended her by name—they were precisely the sort who employed At

Your Service to make their arrangements when they visited Australia. This was not the first time she'd been handpicked. She was good—no, better than good, she was damn good— at her job.

But now he'd arrived, almost an hour early, catching her on the hop and reawakening a swarm of worries. For several seconds she closed her eyes and breathed deeply until the buzzing stopped and her hands steadied. *Just another client,* she told herself sternly, *with enough money and sense of entitlement to never accept "no" for an answer.*

Feeling calmer but no less curious, Isabelle pressed nearer to the window for a better view of the man emerging from the car downstairs. Absently she turned off her iPod, pulled the buds from her ears. The dance mix had been perfect to keep her moving as she prepared the house for his arrival, but now the breezy beat seemed inappropriate. Something like the theme from *Jaws* would be more fitting.

No.

A sliver of heat pierced her belly as she watched him yawn and stretch his long limbs like a big cat in a patch of sun. Nothing as cold-blooded as a shark. Nothing grey, either. From the sun-goldened tips of his deep brown hair to the toes of his hand-tooled leather loafers, he looked right at home ambling around the forecourt of the Mediterranean-style villa. His entrance music would be Ravel…or perhaps a Latin salsa. Something rich and vibrant, thick with the sultry beat of summer. Something befitting a Roman god.

Just another client? An ironic smile touched her lips. *She wished.*

With a name like Cristiano Verón, she should have been prepared for someone slightly more exotic than your average British business tycoon. Instead she'd been distracted by the

British part, by the London address, by the coincidence of timing that brought his booking and request for Isabelle and only Isabelle right after *that* phone call to another London number.

She shook her head and reassured herself for the trillionth time. *A coincidence, Isabelle. London is a big city.*

Unless Apollo downstairs gave her any reason to think otherwise, she would give him the benefit of the doubt and assume he had nothing to do with Hugh Harrington. She could remain wary without paranoia. Curious without crossing personal boundaries. Watching his arrival was okay. Eyeing his godlike derriere as he leaned into the low-slung car to retrieve his luggage, not so much.

Yet Isabelle could not wrench herself away from the window.

Her fingers curled into the plush fabric of the curtains at her side as he straightened, one modest suitcase in hand, and Isabelle caught her first glimpse of his face. Sharply slanted cheekbones, bold lips, dark aviator shades. Then he turned back to lock up the car, and she wanted more, a longer look, without the sunglasses.

As if that silent wish carried across the courtyard on the fluky autumn breeze, he paused to hook the glasses in the neckline of his chocolate brown sweater. And then he looked up, right at the window where she stood.

Isabelle took a rapid step back. Her heart raced, her backed-up breath released in an audible rush. "He couldn't have known I was watching him," she murmured, shaking her head to clear the shimmering heat. "He couldn't have seen me."

Heart pounding a mile a minute, she ventured a peek beyond the magenta velvet drapes, but he'd disappeared from sight. A ridiculous punch of disappointment hollowed her belly. Slowly her fingers released their grip. Less slowly her brain snapped back into gear.

He'd disappeared because he was striding toward the front entrance. Where she should be, cool and composed and collected, to greet his arrival. Miriam Horton would tear strips from her hide if Cristiano Verón were left cooling his heels on the doorstep. She glanced down at her feet and gave a yelp. Doubly so if she opened the door still wearing her slippers.

Scooping up the matronly shoes supplied with the At Your Service housekeeper's uniform, she bolted for the stairs.

Cristo noticed the woman when he drove through the porte cochere into the open courtyard. Not clearly, but as a distinctly feminine silhouette moving—no, not merely moving, she appeared to be dancing—past a window on the house's upper storey.

Sensing it was Isabelle Browne, he felt a sharp kick of anticipation. Suddenly the long trip and the business he'd spent his flight time rescheduling faded to a pin spot. Everything homed in on the woman inside the house.

When he'd discovered that At Your Service was a private concierge service favoured by the wealthy of Melbourne and their international visitors, he had found a possible link to Hugh Harrington. Tenuous, but hunches generally served him well. After contracting the agency to secure a house for his Melbourne stay, he'd tossed out the name Isabelle Browne as a recommendation from a friend. And struck pay dirt.

"I'm afraid Ms. Browne is on leave," the manager explained apologetically. "However, we do have other housekeepers with excellent references."

"Unless Ms. Browne is on sick leave," Cristo said, fishing for further information, "perhaps she could be persuaded to take this job."

"I'm sorry, Mr. Verón, but she has already turned down a position this week."

"Did that position offer double her usual wage?"

Money, as always, spoke with the sweetest of tongues. Less than an hour later, Cristo received a return call from At Your Service. He had his housekeeper of choice.

He also had a plan, one that followed the old adage about catching more flies with honey than with vinegar. By befriending her and asking the right questions, he would uncover what he needed to know about her alleged relationship with Hugh. Perhaps Isabelle Browne had worked as his housekeeper, perhaps for a house party he'd attended. Perhaps he didn't recognise her name because he hadn't bothered to ask.

As he pulled his luggage from the car, he sensed her scrutiny from an upstairs window. And he couldn't help wondering if she'd subjected Hugh to the same covert once-over. If she'd sized him up as potential prey for a pregnancy trap.

When he turned toward the house, he couldn't resist lifting his gaze to the window. He could no longer see her, but he knew she was there, watching him from behind the window's heavy frame of curtains. The hum of anticipation in his blood changed tenor, sharpening with a new intent.

Perhaps a more active approach would better serve his purpose. Patience, to his way of thinking, was an overrated virtue.

"Perhaps, Ms. Isabelle Browne—" his narrowed gaze raked the window one last time, and a faint smile ghosted across his lips as he strode toward the portico "—you are about to get more than you bargained for."

Two

At the airfield, Cristo had collected keys, car, directions and a large helping of flattery from the At Your Service manager. He'd wasted enough time deflecting that; he didn't intend wasting any more standing around beneath the portico. When his first press of the doorbell went unanswered, he used the supplied key. The heavy door swung open smoothly and silently, and he stepped into the foyer.

A woman—Isabelle Browne, he presumed—stood at the foot of the stairs. Poised on one leg, one hand on the banister for balance, she appeared to be midway through changing her shoes. That seemed the logical explanation for the mismatched pairing of one utilitarian lace-up and one sheepskin slipper.

The second shoe, in her hand, disappeared behind her back as she straightened. Standing on the short side of average, that did not take her long. Cristo allowed himself significantly longer to take her all in.

She was pretty in a wholesome, girl-next-door way. Sandy blond hair scraped back from her face revealed a high, smooth forehead and wide, startled eyes. Cheeks flushed, lips parted on a note of surprise, no makeup as far as he could tell. As for her body…he could tell even less. She wore an unflattering housekeeper's uniform, complete with starched apron.

She did not look like a temptress.

She did not look like Hugh Harrington's type at all.

When his gaze returned to her face, Cristo noted the hint of annoyance now glimmering in her eyes. Because of his long, leisurely perusal? Or because he'd caught her out?

"Welcome to Pelican Point, Mr. Verón," she said, releasing her grip on the banister and dipping into an awkward bob. The hand holding the shoe remained out of sight. "I am so sorry I wasn't downstairs to greet you at the door."

Professional obsequiousness, Cristo decided, did not suit a woman wearing mismatched shoes and an expression of barely disguised irritation.

"There's no need to apologise. As you can see, I am quite capable of opening—" he paused to kick the door shut behind him "—and closing the door."

"Of course, but one of my duties is to greet guests."

"I am happy for you to greet me here." Cristo closed the space between them in half a dozen unhurried strides. He extended his free hand along with a winning smile. "I am Cristo Verón."

Ignoring both his proffered hand and the smile, she ducked her head in acknowledgement. "May I take your bag, Mr. Verón?"

When she made a move toward his suitcase, he angled his body to block her path. Her hand grazed his flank, and she snatched it away. Her face pinkened into an unmistakable blush.

Had *she* felt that crackle of contact, too? Interesting.

"I'm sorry, Mr. Ver—"

"Please, call me Cristo," he interrupted, putting down his bag. Belatedly he wondered if there'd been a last-minute reassignment of staff. If Ms. Browne had changed her mind, or if her delicate condition meant she'd needed to pass up the sweet deal he'd offered for her services. "And you are Isabelle?"

"Ms. Browne."

So, no mistake. No changed arrangement. A pity, Cristo decided, because Ms. Browne wasn't anything like the woman he'd expected.

"Isn't that a little formal?" he asked.

"At Your Service prefers formality," she replied, as prim and starched as her attire.

"But what about you, Isabelle? Do you prefer this formality?" He gestured at the unfortunate grey uniform as he slowly circled her still, straight-backed form. Idly he recalled his impression of her dancing past the window, the swing of an arm and the bump of her hips. Then he leaned down to retrieve the discarded slipper from the bottom step. "Or is this more to your liking?"

"It doesn't matter whether I like the uniform," she replied, a bite of pique in both her voice and her eyes, "but I do have to wear it."

"What if I prefer a more casual dress code?"

What looked like suspicion flickered across her face before she looked down at the shapeless dress. "I would have to ask what is wrong with this. It is supplied and serviceable and…and…"

"Ugly?" he supplied helpfully when she struggled for description.

Surprise brought her head up, and their eyes met for a

moment, hers warm with suppressed humour. The transformation was remarkable. Cristo couldn't help but contemplate the effect of her full smile on an unsuspecting male.

"I was going to say comfortable," she said.

"Even the footwear?"

Consternation chased the smile from her eyes. "I'm sorry. I wasn't expecting you so soon. I didn't expect you would let yourself in. I—"

She pressed her lips together, shutting off the hurried defence. Her weight shifted from one mismatched foot to the other, and he could tell she was annoyed with herself for being drawn into an explanation. Probably contravened the rules of formality.

Cristo held out the slipper. "If these are more comfortable, wear them," he said, leaning forward to smile confidingly as he captured her gaze. He dropped his voice a half note. "I won't tell."

For a long moment she didn't do anything but blink, several slow sweeps of her silky dark lashes that failed to disguise the confusion in her hazel eyes. He really had thrown her. She really was nothing like he'd expected.

"All right." Despite the husky uncertainty in her voice, she gave a businesslike nod and straightened her shoulders. "Would you like me to show you through the house now?"

"By all means," Cristo said equitably. "Just as soon as you finish making your feet comfortable."

Call-me-Cristo Verón was nothing like the usual At Your Service client, Isabelle thought gloomily as she scuttled downstairs thirty minutes later. The thing with her uniform and shoes was only the start. During their tour of the spacious house he'd been all polite attention, but she'd felt a significant proportion of that attention concentrated on her rather than the features and fixtures she pointed out.

She'd never been more acutely aware of a client in ten-plus years of housekeeping. She'd never been more aware of a man in all her twenty-eight years. From the instant he'd come through the front door and caught her balancing on one leg like some kind of demented flamingo, he'd kept her off-balance.

It was more than being caught out by his unheralded entry and more than her curiosity about why he'd requested her as his only domestic. More even than his outrageously good looks, because there, too, he'd gone and thrown her. Up close the bump of an old break marred the strong line of his nose and a scar cut through one eyebrow.

Small imperfections that balanced the sensual beauty of his perfectly formed mouth and the rich underbelly of his voice.

Small reminders that he was not a god but a man.

Not just any man, Isabelle reminded herself, but a client. She had no business getting in a lather over that dark-honey voice or the way he softened the *s* in her name. Even if he weren't a client, she had no business. Her whole life was in flux at the moment. She'd taken time off work to sort out *what next,* but then she hadn't been able to refuse the money attached to this job.

Sure she'd been worried and wary, but she could not have anticipated this unlikely attraction. A heavy sigh escaped her lips. She'd been fine, relatively speaking, while he kept his distance. But then he would stand a little too near or look at her a little too long and her hormones would start dancing around in silly, look-at-me excitement. Reflexively she touched a hand to dance central, low in her belly. There'd been too many of those moments, when she'd forgotten her professional house-keeper's spiel and stumbled over her words. Or her feet.

The last she'd done just now in her rush to exit his bedroom. He'd started to pull off his sweater en route to the bathroom and that glimpse of lithe muscles and olive skin and silky, dark chest hair was more than enough for her imagination. She didn't need to view any more interesting facets of Cristo Verón, thank you very much!

The man was unpredictable…dangerously so.

"It will be okay," she told herself, fanning her hot face with a rapidly flapping hand as she turned into the kitchen. Her sanctuary. Her centre. "He's here for a week. Of business."

Isabelle knew the corporate drill. Long meetings, restaurant meals; often she went days barely sighting her clients. She just needed a little time to get used to him and his overly familiar ways.

Was he flirting? Oh, yes. Isabelle had no doubts on that score, but Cristo Verón struck her as the type who flirted in his sleep. Just like she was going through the motions now, piping the mixture she'd prepared earlier into delicate petits fours. Sliding the perfectly aligned baking sheets into the oven.

Isabelle baked on autopilot; Cristo Verón flirted.

The insight cheered her. She set the timer and wiped the countertop until the quartz gleamed. In her kitchen, she was in control and all was right with the world. Now she'd acknowledged the attraction for what it was—she was female; how could she not respond?—she could handle Cristiano Verón and whatever he threw at her next…as long as that wasn't another article of clothing.

Rattled by the possibility of a complete striptease, Isabelle had fled his bedroom suite without asking if he preferred coffee or tea. She made both. She set the table in the breakfast nook that offered a spectacular view over Port Phillip Bay, and by the time she heard his firm tread crossing the parlour, she'd laid out a spread of roast beef and cress sandwiches, almond biscotti and lemon shortbread. The Swiss cakes were cooling on the benchtop. Everything looked perfect.

She wiped her hands, straightened her apron and drew a deep breath. This time she would act like a poised professional if it killed her. No stuttering, no staring, no stumbling.

He came through the archway via the wet bar: appropriately, since his hair was still slick from the shower. Wet and dark and longer than she'd realised. The ends grazed his collar and the front still bore the marks of his comb.

There was something indefinably intimate about that glimpse into his grooming, about knowing that minutes earlier he'd stood naked beneath a shower jet. Now he wore harmless dark trousers and a pure white shirt, but her insides tightened impurely, ambushed by bare-and-wet-skinned images. To her credit, Isabelle didn't stare, not at his freshly shaven jaw nor at the flare of his nostrils as he breathed in the scent of her baking. But then he picked up a petit four from the cooling tray and juggled it from one hand to the other as if judging the temperature, and that contrast of large, olive-skinned hands and tiny, delicate cake held her riveted.

Then he popped it in his mouth and murmured something low and indistinguishable and possibly foreign. Exact words didn't matter. His meaning was clear in the warm glimmer of his eyes and in the little finger-kissing gesture that followed.

It was very European and immensely flattering, and the way her hormones danced around in giddy response sounded a loud, clanging alarm in Isabelle's brain. She shook herself back into the real world, where the housekeeper didn't stare at her employer's hands and mouth and fantasise about that kiss on her skin.

When he reached for a second cake, she slid the tray out of reach.

"Is that silent chastisement?" he asked, smiling, unchastised. "Or is there a one-treat limit?"

She couldn't look at that smile; it would tie her tongue in knots. With quick hands, she transferred the remaining cakes to a serving plate, then slid it across the countertop. "Go your hardest," she invited.

One brow rose in a questioning arch. A wicked glint darkened his eyes. Isabelle gave herself a silent scolding. Obviously she needed to be on her mettle, to watch her tongue, to measure her words.

"They are all for you," she said more carefully. "And those." She gestured to the table at his back. "Would you prefer tea or coffee?"

Casting a quick eye over the offerings, he didn't address the question. Instead he asked, "Did you make the biscotti, Isabelle?"

His mouth turned the words over like a slow caress, and Isabelle caught herself watching, fascinated, for a second too long. For distraction she turned to the teapot. Whether he wanted tea or not, the measured actions gave her something to concentrate on other than the illusive wisp of an accent in his voice. She longed to ask about that, told herself it was not hers to know.

"Yes," she managed to answer. "They're all homemade." From the corner of her eye she saw him moving, not taking a seat at the table, but settling his hips against the countertop. His watchful silence was so unsettling that she found herself adding, "The biscotti is my gran's recipe."

"Did she teach you to bake?"

"She taught me everything."

It was a simple statement but so full of truth that Isabelle regretted opening her mouth. Not talking about herself, being just another efficient but invisible tool in a well-stocked household, was one of the things she liked about this job. That and the cooking-in-fabulously-equipped-kitchens part. "Would now be a good time to discuss menus?" she asked.

"What do you need to know?" he responded, still watching her instead of the menus she fanned out on the countertop. Still taking up too much space, his direct, dark-eyed gaze made her feel all too visible.

"It will help my planning if I know your schedule," Isabelle said. "I prefer notice on which meals you require me to cook, when you will be eating out, if you're expecting guests."

"Tonight I am eating out. I have a meeting in—" he shot a cuff and consulted an expensive-looking watch "—fifty minutes."

"Where is your meeting?" she asked automatically. "At this time of day, it will take more than an hour to drive into the city."

"Not the city. Brighton. It sounds as though you have a good local knowledge."

"I am a local. Do you need directions? I have a street directory in—"

"Thank you, but not necessary. My car has sat nav."

Of course it did. Isabelle gave herself a swift mental kick. She'd been too intent on the man, had barely noticed the car. No doubt it was as sleek, expensive and European as its driver.

"Would forty minutes be sufficient driving time?" he asked.

"I'd allow forty-five, minimum, to be sure."

Somehow he'd managed to trap her gaze, to hold it with the steady strength of his. "Is that your way, Isabelle? Are you the careful type who always makes allowances for the unexpected?"

"I believe that is efficient," she said carefully. "And sensible."

"Like your sensible and efficient uniform?"

Not really, but she did not want to indulge whatever issue he had with formality. The shapeless grey dress might be ugly, but it suited Isabelle just fine. "About the menus. Could we look at your preferences?"

She slid the breakfast list forward; he gave it one perfunctory glance and slid it back. "Juice, orange. Eggs, poached. Bacon, crisp but not too crispy. Coffee, Colombian, black."

So, he could *address the question efficiently when he chose to. Praise be.* "And lunch tomorrow?"

This time he didn't even glance at the menu choices. "Let's wing it."

"Wing it?" She frowned. "You must have some requirements, some preferences."

"Only one." With fluid grace he straightened his negligent posture and touched her Peter Pan collar with the knuckles of one hand. "This has to go."

"But I'm required to—"

"I would think that I am paying you enough to entitle me to dictate my own requirements, don't you?"

Isabelle nodded stiffly, then swallowed. He was too close, in her space. An insidious warmth pooled in her belly and thickened her voice when she spoke. "What are your requirements, Mr. Verón?"

"For a start, I don't stand on ceremony. There is no need to address me as Mr. Verón."

"But—"

He silenced her objection with a finger to her lips. "My name is Cristo. Let us start with that and work our way up, shall we?"

Shocked by his unexpected touch, fighting the temptation to lean into it, to open her mouth, Isabelle stared up at him for a full second before she could process the request and voice any form of response. "I can try," she said huskily.

"You strike me as very capable, Isabelle. I'm sure you will catch on."

Isabelle wasn't sure she wanted to catch on to something that involved the intimacy of first names and working their way up. But as he'd pointed out, he was the boss and paying her an obscenely generous wage, so she nodded in reluctant agreement. And focussed on the lesser of two evils. "What do you require me to wear instead of this uniform?"

"Whatever is comfortable," he said after considering the question far longer than it warranted. "As long as it is not grey."

Not grey Isabelle could do, but comfortable? No, she couldn't imagine ever being comfortable with this man. Not when her body still simmered from that simple glancing touch to her lips. Not after his sleepy-lidded eyes had glimmered with wicked intent while he considered the question of her work attire.

Was he picturing her without the uniform? Or in some sexy male-fantasy version? The possibilities should have appalled her, but instead they blazed in her mind as she watched him walk away.

His walk, like so much else about Cristo Verón, was confident and captivating. It grabbed her attention and didn't let go until the front door shut in his wake. Damn the man. He was like some sexy, six-foot, treacle-voiced magnetic field.

Isabelle should have been pleased to see the back of him, but after releasing the breath backed up in her lungs, she slumped into a chair. It was as though his departure had sucked the life force from the air and the stuffing from her legs. Ridiculous, she told herself. And when she ran that last exchange back over, she kicked herself for the missed opportunity.

If she'd been on her game, she would have asked *why* he was paying her the extravagant wage. Who had recommended her so glowingly that he would accept no substitute? Those were not questions she could ask Miriam Horton. At Your Service had a strict policy on discussing clients, but given that the client himself had brought it up, she could have angled in a polite query. Especially since he was pushing for informality in their working relationship. Next time the subject came up, she would not miss the opportunity.

Fortified by that decision, she cleared away the untouched afternoon-tea spread and did a run to the shops for breakfast supplies. Specifically, his requested blend of coffee. She thought about circling around to her home. It was only a ten-minute drive, and she could pick up some comfortable, non-grey clothes. It wasn't as though she needed to be in situ tonight. She didn't expect she would see her client—she could not bring herself to think of him as Cristo—again until breakfast.

But then she thought about her sister and the questions she was likely to ask, and turned her car back toward Mt Eliza. Tomorrow would be soon enough to face Chessie's inquisition.

She should have known her sister better.

Her call came late. No greeting, just an economical "Well?"

Isabelle didn't need any further explanation. They'd spent a lot of years with only each other; they spoke fluent sisterly shorthand. Chessie wanted details, a blow-by-blow of her first afternoon back at work and her impression of Cristiano Verón, but Isabelle found herself unaccountably shy for words.

"Can you not talk?" Chessie asked into the lengthening silence. "Is he there? Are you still working?"

Isabelle contemplated taking the coward's way out, but she couldn't do it. She couldn't lie to Chessie; she could only pre-varicate. "No, he's not here, but I don't have anything to report. He arrived this afternoon and went out to a business meeting soon after."

"And?" Chessie persisted. "You must have formed some impression."

A tumult of impressions tumbled over each other in Isabelle's mind, but only one singled itself out as relevant. "He's exactly like his name." Exotic, expensive, exclusively designer label. "He is Cristiano Verón."

"You did it? You took my advice and checked his passport?" Chessie sounded both shocked and impressed. "Outstanding!"

Isabelle pinched the bridge of her nose. "I did not look through his things," she said tightly. "I do not want to lose my job."

"You sounded so certain."

"I am. Don't ask me why, just trust my instincts on this," she said, struggling to sound reassuring when her stomach churned with uncertainty. She could have shared those feelings, but then Chessie was such a wild card. Isabelle did not need her arriving to suss the situation in her impulsive, to-hell-with-the-consequences way. She'd jeopardised Isabelle's position with At Your Service once already; she was not allowing her a second chance. "One thing I do know, he is not Hugh Harrington."

"That doesn't mean he's not a lackey," Chessie countered.

Releasing a short, humourless laugh, Isabelle shook her head. "Believe me, Chess, Cristiano Verón is nobody's lackey. I really do think this is a coincidence of timing, that he's a genuine client here on business. Anyone could have recommended me. The Thompsons, for a start."

"If you say so," Chessie said with a distinct lack of conviction.

"I *do* say so. And if anything happens that changes my mind, you will be the first to know."

Three

Was she pregnant?

From the entryway to the kitchen Cristo eyed his house-keeper's profile as she stretched to open an overhead cupboard. How in the name of all that was sacred could he tell when she insisted on wearing that sack of a dress? Today's version was not grey but an equally dull brown.

What kind of woman elected to wear something so unflattering when she had the go-ahead to choose anything she liked? One who honoured her rules of employment so rigidly that she would not risk her boss's censure? One who took pleasure in countermanding his request for informality?

Or one who didn't want to draw attention to a thickened waistline?

Cristo watched her cross the kitchen with a shimmy in her walk. She looked spry, not pale, with the effects of morning sickness. As she scooped coffee into the machine, she threw in a loose-jointed sway of her hips that turned his mouth dry. She was singing, too, in a disjointed but warmly tuneful one-word-here, one-hum-there manner that teased his lips into a smile that was quickly quashed. He did not want to be charmed by her or distracted from his purpose, and yet in the past two days she'd evaded his every effort at casual get-to-know-you conversation.

Today was Saturday. Time to step up the pressure.

Absorbed in her breakfast preparations, she still hadn't noticed him in the doorway, and when she stretched higher still, reaching into the overhead cupboard, he seized the opportunity to reveal his presence.

"Let me get that for you."

With a startled shriek she dropped the bowl, and Cristo hurried to steady her. His reaction was unnecessary, the placement of his hands on the soft curve between waist and hips deliberate, but then he looked down and lost himself in her deepwater eyes. On first meeting he'd thought them hazel, but he'd been wrong. Wrong, too, when he'd judged her merely pretty. That description did Isabelle Browne quite an injustice.

"I'm fine now," she said in a strangled voice. "Please take your hands off me."

Slowly Cristo released his grip. He took an equally measured step away. The impression of giving female flesh tingled in his palms as he held them up in a gesture of truce, but his attention was all on her hands that trembled visibly as she ripped earbuds from her ears and tossed them with her music device onto the countertop.

"I'm sorry for startling you." He dipped his head apologetically. "I didn't realise that you couldn't hear my offer to help." He'd been too intent on inspecting her waistline, and then on watching her dance moves, when he should have considered the source of the singing and dancing.

"You scared several years off my life." Her nostrils flared slightly as she drew a breath and let it go. Still rattled, but making a valiant effort to regather her composure. "You mentioned a later breakfast today. I didn't expect to see you downstairs this early."

"I'm a morning person. Waking early is a habit. I've been working for a while…as have you, it would seem." Cristo gestured at the evidence of her early morning industry. The fruit neatly cut. The coffee brewing. The oven's low hum and the sweet aroma of baking.

"My favourite time of day," she admitted. "I like the peace and the solitude. I can work to my own rhythm."

He arched a brow at her abandoned iPod, and Isabelle winced.

Had she been singing out loud? First the slippers and now impromptu karaoke. Talk about your consummate professional!

From now on she would be all business, all of the time.

"Your breakfast won't be long." Briskly she moved to the stove. Switched on the flame. "The morning papers are on the table, which I've set by the window. There are also two phone messages I took last night. If you would care to take a seat, I will bring your coffee."

In her peripheral vision she saw him glance toward the table, and willed him to follow the glance with his feet. How could she have been oblivious to his arrival? Fresh from his morning shower, he wore jeans—designer label, no doubt—and a black sweater that could, quite conceivably, be cashmere or silk or something equally delicate and soft to the touch. He, on the other hand, looked big and strong and completely male.

And she could still feel the imprint of his hands at her waist.

"With the coffee, please bring a second cup."

The unexpected request snapped Isabelle back to attention. "Will your guest be staying for breakfast?" she asked, and somehow she managed to sound polite, professional, unperturbed.

"My guest?" His dark gaze flicked over her face. "You misunderstand, Isabelle." Perhaps it was her imagination, but his voice seemed to deepen, to caress each note of her name. "The second cup is for you. I would like to discuss my weekend schedule, and I believe your local knowledge will be helpful."

Isabelle insisted on completing his breakfast, which she managed despite the distractingly deep hum of his voice returning one of last night's calls. Which one, she wondered? Vivi's call regarding Amanda's wedding, or Chloe calling about Gisele?

Neither was any of her business; she had no right to stew over that string of exotically feminine names. Even if the spark she felt was mutual, he was the wrong man at completely the wrong time. Yet she remained entirely too aware of him—the pull of worry that drew his brows together, the distracted tap of his fingers against the tabletop, his frowning eyes following her around the kitchen.

By the time she joined him at the table, her nerves were strung like a tightly quivering bow. She hated that he'd made her so self-aware. Especially here in the kitchen, *her* place, where she always felt at ease.

Once he'd established that she had already eaten and, no, she did not want coffee because she had given it up, he asked her to recommend a local restaurant. Isabelle's wariness eased. This was her territory. She settled back in her chair, not exactly relaxed but at least not perched on its lip like a sprinter on the blocks.

"Do you have a preference for any specific style of cuisine?" she asked.

"Good local food, nothing too fancy."

That described her local fish and chips shop, but Isabelle couldn't picture Cristo Verón—even in jeans—eating from a paper bundle on the picnic tables opposite Rosa and Joe's. She figured that her definition of "nothing fancy" might bear little acquaintanceship to his.

"There are a number of winery restaurants on the peninsula which fit that description. Is this for lunch or dinner?"

"Lunch, today. I'm driving to a farm near Geelong this morning to look at ponies. Is there somewhere between there and here, on the return drive?"

"Several," she replied, trying to quell her curiosity over his morning's plans. *Did he have children? Why else would a man look at ponies? But then why would he be looking in Australia?* "They're all very popular at the weekend, so I would suggest making a reservation."

He'd taken the seat facing out onto the terrace and gardens, and the morning sunlight softened eyes she'd thought black to a deep velvety brown. "You will be able to secure us a table at one of these places?"

Isabelle's heart did an anxious flutter before she realised that "us" had nothing to do with her. No doubt he'd be lunching with clients or perhaps his pony-farm friends. "At whichever you choose."

"Which would *you* choose, Isabelle?"

"I couldn't say without more information."

"For you."

Isabelle blinked. "For me?"

Easing back in his chair, he linked his fingers loosely over his chest. "I'm asking which of these restaurants would be your personal choice for lunch."

"None of the above," she admitted. When one dark brow rose

infinitesimally, she quickly added, "Not because I wouldn't want to eat there, but because they're not within my means."

"If you had the means?"

"Acacia Ridge." She named her wish-list number one without hesitation. "Their menu uses local produce in simple dishes with a twist. The cellar is legendary, the service superb and the outlook makes you forget you're so near the city."

"It sounds like a favourite."

"I've never eaten there, but it's a favourite with clients."

"We shall have to do something about that omission," he said easily, "so you can speak from firsthand knowledge."

"Perhaps I will treat myself after this week," she replied, although she knew there would be no treats. Her pay was earmarked for practical purposes, like medical bills and nursery essentials. "I have holiday time due," she added.

"Which I believe I interrupted, enticing you to take this job."

Isabelle sat up straighter. Unwittingly she had turned the conversation around and provided the perfect opening. Her heart rate kicked up, and she took a second to compose herself, striving to appear relaxed as she prepared the questions she'd been dying to ask. "If you don't mind me asking… Why did you do that? Why did you request me as your housekeeper?"

"Your name came up when I was talking to a friend." The hitch of one shoulder was elegantly nonchalant. "Why do you ask?"

Isabelle considered how to answer. She could hardly say: *Because I was wondering if you have some connection to Hugh Harrington, if you're here in response to an I'm-pregnant phone call, possibly to make that inconvenience go away.*

"Did you think the request unusual?" he continued when she didn't answer right away. "I find it hard to believe that this level of service—" his small gesture took in the table setting, the daffodils she'd picked fresh at dawn, the basket of cinnamon scrolls fresh from her oven and the coffee tray with milk in three strengths and four choices of sweetening "—would not earn you many glowing recommendations."

"Yes," she admitted, "but never for such a generous wage."

"You were on leave, presumably with holiday plans in place. I wanted to ensure my offer covered the inconvenience and made it worth your while. I interpreted your acceptance as meaning I had offered sufficient incentive and compensation." His gaze fixed on hers, no longer sleepy-lidded but direct and steady. "Am I to believe I was wrong?"

He thought she was complaining about the pay? "No," she replied adamantly, heat bleeding into her face at the thought. "You are paying me far too much to do far too little!"

"Then perhaps I need to look at increasing your workload."

"Of course," she said hurriedly. "Whatever you require. I would appreciate the chance to earn my pay."

For several seconds he seemed to consider that offer, his fingers linked loosely while his thumbs drummed a relaxed rhythm against his black-sweatered chest. But his eyes on hers were intent, and the mood had changed subtly, indescribably. "Do you have anything specific in mind?" he asked.

Isabelle felt a tightening in her skin. Awareness, she thought, that had nothing to do with business and everything to do with the undercurrents in that question. Her mind hazed over for a second of very specific images—*his hands, her waist, no black sweater, no ugly uniform*—and she had to clear the heat from her synapses before she could construct a businesslike answer. "Cooking is what I do best. If you have any special requests, or perhaps you might care to invite your business associates or friends here for dinner rather than a restaurant. I've also been called upon to shop. If there's anything you need for yourself or as a gift for your…anyone," she finished lamely.

One dark brow arched mockingly. "My…anyone?"

"Your wife," she supplied tartly, thinking of all those damned names on the phone messages again, "or your mistress. Sometimes I've shopped for both."

"Messy."

"I wouldn't know."

"Fortunately," he said slowly after a beat of pause, "I have neither."

She could do nothing to stop the absurd leap of gladness, nothing except pray it didn't show in her expression. His personal life was not her concern; she did not want to know about Vivi and company. No, she did not.

"No shopping and no dinner parties," he said, "but I do have something else in mind. Do you drive?"

"Yes, I do."

"Can you be ready to leave in half an hour?"

Isabelle felt as though she was being led blindfolded toward the cliff edge, but what could she do? She'd offered to earn her pay; it was too late to rescind the offer. She moistened her suddenly dry lips and plunged ahead. "Yes."

"Good," he said with a businesslike nod, and for a brief second Isabelle's qualms settled. He was sending her on an errand. A task to fill in part of a day that would otherwise be spent dusting and vacuuming a spotless house.

"Where will I be going?" she asked. "Do I need to change?"

"Out of that?" He favoured her uniform with a look of high disdain. "Please do."

"I don't have anything but jeans."

"Which will be fine for where we're going."

"We?"

In the process of refilling his coffee, he paused to capture her startled gaze. His was heavy-lidded, dark and languorous like his voice. "Did I not make myself clear? You, Isabelle, are driving me to Geelong."

No, that had not been clear, and looking into his unapologetic eyes she sensed that he knew it. What she didn't understand was why, and perhaps that showed in her face.

"I spent most of the last few nights on the phone and computer, working London hours. If I happen to doze off today, I would prefer that I were not behind the wheel."

"I can find you a professional driver," she suggested, searching for a way out.

"Why would I want a professional when I have you, Isabelle?" He unfolded his long frame and pushed to his feet. A hint of amusement glinted in his eyes. "There is no need to look so put-upon. In return for your chauffeuring duties, I am taking you to lunch at this restaurant you speak so highly of."

"I can't go to lunch with you," she choked out.

"Why not? Do you suspect I have ulterior motives? Is that why you questioned my reason for hiring you?" His gaze narrowed on the guilty heat flooding her face, and his voice dropped to a low, insulted tone. "What, exactly, do you think I am paying you for, Isabelle?"

"No, not that," she responded swiftly, but the warmth seeped from her face into her flesh as his meaning took vivid root in her imagination. "I don't expect you would ever need to pay."

His eyebrows shot up.

"I mean for a woman's company…to coax a woman to spend time in your company." Could she make a worse hash of explaining herself? She drew a deep breath and, avoiding the intent interest—and some amusement—in his eyes, smoothed her hands down her thighs before continuing in a less flustered tone. "You know what I mean, but that isn't why I'm squeamish about going to lunch with you."

"So, there is another reason?"

"I am the housekeeper."

"My housekeeper," he corrected, "who stated that she isn't doing enough to earn her pay. To make up for that, I have appointed you as my driver for today. Since I will be stopping for lunch, I am asking you to join me. If it helps, perhaps you can consider it professional development."

Four

"Is the menu not up to your expectations, Isabelle?"

In the hours spent crossing the bay by ferry, driving to the Armitage polo stables and then returning to the restaurant, Cristo hadn't dozed off in the passenger seat. He'd pressed his driver-for-the-day into conversation, asking about the sites they passed, about the local foods and wines, about driving and the rented Porsche that had caused her much I-can't-drive-this! trepidation at first. Deliberate topics that weren't too personal, that encouraged her to drop the professional reticence and relax in his company, and with her occupied behind the wheel Cristo was able to study the fine nuances of her expression. She gave away a lot with the set of her brows, by holding her mouth a certain way, or by distractedly chewing at her bottom lip.

"The menu is wonderful," she said now in answer to his question, but Cristo shook his head.

"You say it's wonderful, but you were worrying away at your lip—" he tapped a finger against his own bottom lip, indicating the exact spot where she habitually snagged the plushest point of hers "—just there."

"That is lack of orthodontic intervention, not a critique of the menu."

Cristo laughed softly at her quick answer. She'd surprised him many times this morning with her sharp observations once he'd encouraged her to say what she thought rather than what she thought was expected. The biggest surprise: how much he liked the real Isabelle he saw emerging from behind the polite, professional housekeeper. "In which case I applaud the lack of intervention."

"You prefer crooked teeth?" she asked, eyebrows rising with scepticism.

"Imperfections lend a face interest."

For a second she stared back at him. Then she shook her head, just once, and expelled an incredulous breath. "Suggesting that someone has an *interesting* face is not exactly flattering."

"And here I was thinking you would scoff at flattery," Cristo countered idly, but when their eyes met and held he sensed a new element in her regard. Surprise at his observation, yes, but also an acknowledgement that bordered on approval. For the first time he felt her honest response to him as a man, and he allowed himself to enjoy the elemental attraction that buzzed between them in that rare unguarded moment.

No harm, he told himself, since he fully intended to use that attraction to his own ends. "You strike me as a straightforward woman," he said.

"A straightforward woman with crooked teeth."

Entertained by the quick comeback, Cristo lolled back in his chair and allowed his gaze to drift to her lips. Full, plush, unenhanced by any cosmetic products as far as he could tell. And their softened set revealed a hint of those not-quite-straight teeth that he found so unexpectedly appealing. "You don't find flaws interesting?" he asked.

"That would depend on the story behind the flaw. My teeth, for example—" her tongue appeared to trace their underside, an innocent gesture that caused a not-so-innocent stirring low in Cristo's body "—just grew this way. Nothing of interest there."

"Your opinion."

Their gazes linked again, a moment longer, a spark warmer. "Is there a story behind your broken nose?" she asked.

"Not a particularly interesting one."

"Your opinion."

This time he laughed out loud. She was sharp. The kind of woman he would take a keen interest in pursuing, if she were any other woman. "The result of a fall from a horse," he admitted.

"You're kidding!"

He favoured her with an amused look. "If I intended inventing a tale, I would make it a trifle more heroic…or at least wild and daring. Sadly, it was the result of my backside and saddle parting company."

"After watching your b…*you,*" she corrected hastily, "this morning, I couldn't imagine you ever parting company with your saddle."

"So, you *were* watching."

Primitive male satisfaction drummed through Cristo as he observed the pretty flush that rose from her throat and into her face. "Yes," she admitted, "but I know nothing about polo. I didn't know you call the horses you ride ponies, for example." Then, after a beat of pause, "I suppose you were born with a silver polo stick in your hand."

Cristo laughed, low and genuinely entertained. "Not quite.

My father played professionally, so I was born with the scent of hay and horsehair in my blood if not quite wielding a mallet. I doubt my mother would have allowed that."

"She isn't into polo?"

"She had a passing fascination with the men who played," he supplied dryly. "Something about the Argentinean flair, I believe."

"I see."

The words were drawn out, thoughtful, and Cristo's gaze narrowed on hers. "What is it that you see, Isabelle?"

"Your name, your looks… I thought you might be Italian."

"Partly, although those genes are from my mother."

"She's Italian?"

"Vivi is half Italian, half English. All crazy."

Her eyes livened with interest, but he saw her rein that curiosity in. Her lips pressed together in self-restraint. Because family interest was getting too personal?

Too bad, Isabelle Browne. As far as personal goes, I'm only getting started.

"My father is Argentinean," he said, continuing from where he'd left off. Selective pieces of his personal story would serve as encouragement for when he zeroed in on hers. "Although my mother's second husband was more of a father to me."

"Is he English?" she asked after a moment, giving in to the curiosity that glowed bright in her eyes.

"Proudly. When he promoted Chisholm Air internationally, Alistair played shamelessly on every cliché of the English aristocracy."

"Alistair Chisholm," she asked with rising wonderment, "is your stepfather?"

"Was."

"Of course, I read about his death in the papers. I'm sorry."

"As am I," Cristo said. "My mother's best choice of husbands by far."

"So, you moved from Argentina to England?" she asked after a moment's reflection.

"And then to Italy after my mother's third marriage, and then back to my father's estancia for several years. That's where this happened."

He grazed a thumb lazily down the slope of his nose, saw Isabelle follow the action with reluctant interest in her eyes. She moistened her lips. "How?"

"On a dare from my brother, I took on an unbroken mare with an evil nature. Evil won."

"Machismo," she intoned, although the disapproving tone didn't quite ring true. Not with inquisitive interest glowing bright in her eyes. "Serves you right."

"The pain to my pride was considerable, but the sympathy I received more than made up for it."

"Female sympathy, I presume."

Cristo grinned lazily. "Is there any other kind?"

She let go a laugh full of disbelief, yet it still managed to slide under his skin. Beyond the nimbus of her hair—at some point of the morning the thick curls had sprung free of their usual ponytail restraint—he saw their waitress approaching, but he delayed her with the barest of signals. "What about you, Isabelle Browne with an *e*," he asked, deliberately choosing the phrase Hugh had quoted from her phone call. But he saw nothing in her eyes except lively amusement. "Have you lived around here for a long time?"

"I've lived in Melbourne most of my life, and here on the peninsula for the past six years."

"You really are a local."

"Yep." The smile in her eyes teased the corners of her mouth and tickled his libido. "In the past twenty years I haven't been any farther than one holiday to Bali."

"You have no ambition to see the world?"

"Oh, I'd love to travel, but I'm afraid that ambition has been put on hold. At the moment I have other priorities."

She spoke evenly, furnishing the information with matter-of-fact ease, but there was something going on behind her eyes and a tension in the edges of her smile. *Other priorities.* That could encompass a multitude of possibilities, but one blared loud in Cristo's mind.

Pregnancy.

The reminder of what had brought them to this place, this conversation, chilled the relaxed heat in his veins. He'd not forgotten his purpose, but he'd allowed his enjoyment of her company to colour his perception. No more. Straightening in his seat, he signalled the waitress. "We should order. What do you fancy?"

The worry creases between her brows deepened as she scanned the menu again. "Everything is so…much."

Everything was exactly as she'd described it that morning—simple ingredients, with a twist. "Do you mean the prices?" he asked, taking a second look before shrugging dismissively. "Compared with London, these are modest."

"Perhaps for you," she murmured.

"Since I'm paying, let's not make it a problem for you." He reached across and removed the menu from her hand. Leaning back in his chair, he smiled at the waitress. "What do you recommend, Kate?"

He took control of the ordering with the confident command Isabelle expected of a man from his background. Polo, wealth, privilege. Argentina, England, Italy. No wonder he'd struck her as exotic and expensive. Little wonder he'd taken zero-point-five seconds to charm the waitress, Kate, into a flirtatious smile. The pretty redhead had tripped over herself to assist with wine-matching recommendations along with the food choices.

This all served as a sobering reminder to Isabelle of the vast chasm in their circumstances. The kick she felt low in her belly when he looked at her a certain way, when he laughed at something she'd said, when he'd placed a hand low on her back to usher her toward their table—she wasn't used to having a delicious man like Cristo Verón pay attention to her. As he'd pointed out, she was not the type to respond to flattery. Not that she couldn't enjoy the experience, but she was too sensible to forget her place.

This was work, and she took the opportunity to reinforce that fact when the wine arrived. Even after saying she would be sticking to water, Cristo plucked the bottle from the ice bucket with an aim to pouring for her. She placed her hand over the glass and fixed him with a steady look. "I haven't changed my mind."

Apparently he took that as a challenge, because his gaze narrowed on hers. "You do not like my choice?"

"I'm sure it is a very fine choice—" after all of the confab between him and Kate, how could it not be? "—but I don't drink when I'm working."

"Surely one glass would not hurt."

"Surely you don't mean to tempt me when I'm acting as your driver."

For a long moment their gazes clashed, and she wondered if the dark intensity of his was a response to being thwarted. She couldn't imagine he heard *no* too often. But he did put down the wine, and in his eyes she read a measure of respect. "You do take your job seriously, don't you?"

"Of course," she replied briskly, sitting up straighter and folding her hands neatly in her lap as some sort of counter-foil to the pleasure his approval generated. "At Your Service would not employ me if I didn't."

"Do you like the job?"

"It's a good job."

"But do you *like* it?" he countered, his subtle emphasis demonstrating the distinction between the question he asked and the one she had answered.

"There are aspects I like very much and some I don't," she said carefully. "As with any job, I imagine."

Their starters arrived, and Isabelle was distracted by the plump prawns dressed in lime and hazelnut. She leaned closer to inhale the flavours and struggled not to drool.

"The cooking, I gather, is the part you like."

His insight brought her gaze up from her plate, and she didn't bother hiding her smile or the pleasure in her eyes. "You noticed."

"Impossible not to," he said, his mouth slanting into a re-sponsive smile. "If food is your passion, then why do you not cook as a career?"

"Perhaps I would if I could work somewhere like this."

"And you can't…why?"

"Because they're rather selective," she said dryly, "and I don't have the training or qualifications."

"You could put together excellent references from your boss and clients, I imagine. If that is the direction you wished to take."

Isabelle's brow creased into a frown as she played her fork through her dish. How had he managed to home in on the exact question Chessie had been nagging her about for the past year? A question she'd been considering herself until her options had taken on new restrictions. "There is nothing wrong with being a housekeeper, and what I'm doing for At Your Service includes a lot of cooking in brilliantly equipped kitchens." Then, because her chest was tightening with the anxiety that came from thinking of the future and how she would cope, she had to lighten the mood. "Plus the pay and tips can be brilliant, as well."

"And money is important."

"Of course it is." She responded automatically, but then felt the weight of his gaze on her face. Was he judging her for placing too much importance on her pay packet? How easy for him, in his position. "That is how I pay the bills," she said with more than a touch of irritation. "And keep a roof over my head."

"Only your head, Isabelle?"

He asked easily enough, but there was something in his stillness and quiet attention that set her suspicions alight. Driving to the restaurant he'd said he was starving, yet he'd barely looked at his plate. Something was on his mind. This was more than small talk.

Frown deepening, Isabelle put down her fork and met his gaze. "What are you asking, exactly?"

"Only if you live alone," he replied smoothly. "Yesterday you mentioned a grandmother."

"Gran's been gone for six years."

Even after all those years, memories of Gran caused a thickening of emotion in Isabelle's chest and throat. Perhaps that showed in her voice or her eyes, because Cristo dipped his head slightly, in acknowledgement and perhaps respect for her loss, before asking, "Do you have other family?"

"A sister. We do share a roof," she added. "Just the two of us, at the moment."

The last phrase slipped out before she could stop herself. If she'd not been fixed on his face, drinking from the steady strength of his coal-dark gaze, she might have missed his response.

But she was fixed and she did notice the darkening of his eyes, the tightening in the lines that fanned from their corners, and the concerns he'd almost quashed with the power of his charismatic presence came flooding back. Her heart beat hard in her chest. A new tightness grabbed her by the throat, a mixture of suspicion and protective wariness.

Who are you, Cristiano Verón, and why are you so interested in my family?

From the corner of her eye she saw they were about to be interrupted, not by one of the waitstaff but by a man she pegged as the manager. Their barely touched plates had probably drawn his attention. Isabelle didn't pay complete heed to the man's quiet, apologetic words. *Sorry to interrupt, something about a phone call, yada yada.* Her eyes were trapped hard on Cristo's, awaiting the moment they were alone, while her mind whirred with questions of what to say next.

Could she risk this job, this pay packet from heaven, by confronting him? Perhaps she had imagined his reaction. Perhaps she'd misjudged the reason behind it. Perhaps it would be wise to let the conversation play out until all his cards were on the table….

Then she heard it—the one name guaranteed to snap her to instant, complete attention.

"Mr. Harrington," the manager continued in a sombre tone, "said I should tell you this is urgent and that it concerns Gisele."

Five

Before the manager finished speaking, Cristo had tossed his serviette aside and pushed back his chair. Isabelle's shock registered as a brief flash, like a snapshot taken and stored for later viewing, while his focus homed in on the waiting call.

When at breakfast he'd returned the call from Chloe, his head groom, she had expressed a slight concern over Gisele's lack of appetite. He'd asked her to keep him apprised, but he was unprepared for the grim news delivered by Hugh. The mare's life hung in the balance as a result of acute colic. When Chloe couldn't contact Cristo—he'd turned off his phone, not wanting interruptions to his conversation with Isabelle—in desperation she'd called on Hugh to track him down. They knew he would want to monitor the situation minute by minute. They knew him well.

He cut short their lunch. Then he spent the next five hours with a phone at his ear, talking to his stable staff and the vet, feeling distant and powerless. If getting on a plane could have achieved anything, he would have been airborne right now, taking the fastest route home. But he was a day away from England; the critical stage would have passed long before he arrived. So he returned to Pelican Point, and he paced and he sweated until the final call came through.

The tremendous courage and strength Gisele showed on the polo field had seen her through the worst. The crisis was over. For now she was safe.

A huge wave of relief washed through him, leaving Cristo spent and empty. The perfectly made bed at the centre of the room looked clean and wide and welcoming. Operating on autopilot, he shed his clothes en route to the bathroom. Perhaps it was the sight of that pristine bed or the act of getting naked or the fact that his mind was devoid of all that had occupied it during the long afternoon. Whatever the reason, the picture he'd stowed back at the restaurant suddenly reappeared in full, glossy, living detail.

Isabelle Browne, soft lips parted and eyes wide with shock at the mention of the Harrington name.

Standing with arms braced and hands splayed against the tiles while the shower streamed over the tense muscles of his shoulders and back, Cristo's mind darkened with all the other cues she'd given off over the past days. The baggy uniform. Her refusal to drink coffee or wine. How she'd counted her family as just one sister…at the moment.

There had been no mention of Hugh or their interrupted conversation on the drive home or in the hours since. She'd made several expeditions up the stairs with sandwiches, coffee and finally a dinner tray. He hadn't invited conversation, and she'd resumed her role as invisible housekeeper.

Yet he'd noticed. He'd noticed, and now he quietly seethed

because he'd allowed himself to be taken in by that straight-forward competence and by the other Isabelle with bright interest in her eyes and rhythm in her hips. Both sides attracted him, the antithesis intrigued him, and in that moment of stripped-bare honesty he acknowledged how badly he'd wanted the pregnancy allegation to be a misunderstanding.

If the phone call hadn't interrupted their conversation, he would have asked what she meant by "at the moment"; she would have owned up to impending motherhood; he would have revealed himself as Hugh Harrington's agent. This would be over, done and dusted.

Roughly he towelled himself dry and pulled on a pair of trousers. That was enough for now. On the balcony that surrounded the upper-floor suite of rooms, he dragged the chill air of late autumn into his lungs and welcomed its bite on his exposed chest and arms. Night fell quickly, darkening the waters of the bay and darkening his mind with self-reproach.

Dios, he'd handled this clumsily. He was an arrogant fool for thinking he could judge a woman's character from a few days' observation and one morning of conversation. He was a fool twice over for allowing his desire for the woman a say in that judgement.

Through the French doors came the faint tinkle of spoon against china, and all his senses flared with awareness. She had returned, possibly for the tray, probably with fresh coffee. It was the perfect opportunity to end the subterfuge.

In the doorway he paused, his gaze narrowing as he found her at his desk. Her back was to the door, her head bent forward in apparent concentration, her hands sifting busily through his papers. Suddenly they stopped. Her head came up a fraction as her backbone stiffened.

The burn of awareness in Cristo's blood turned to ice.

"Looking for anything in particular?" he asked, although he knew exactly what she had found.

Heart beating wildly with caught-out shock, Isabelle whipped around and found Cristo standing in the doorway leading to the terrace. He wasn't wearing a shirt. For a long moment the fascinating vista of smooth olive skin over honed muscle drove everything else from her consciousness.

She shouldn't stare. It was wrong to lick one's lips when eyeing one's employer. Wrong to be stung by a prickle of heat and the rampant desire to lick one's employer's chest.

Wrong to be caught red-handed going through his things.

She lifted one of those red hands to her thundering heart. "You have to stop doing that."

The words came in a rush of flustered awareness and guilt as he stepped through the doorway into the full light. "Doing…what?" he asked, his voice as silky as the trail of dark hair bisecting his abdomen.

Must. Not. Stare.

She forced her eyes down—dark trousers, beautifully tailored, perfectly fitted—then up again, all the way to his sleek, wet hair. Although he gave every appearance of relaxation, he wasn't lounging against the doorjamb. She sensed a coiled tension in every long, lean muscle. Like a pampas cat, sizing up his prey and ready to pounce.

A *danger, beware* tremor rippled through her flesh. She pressed her fingers harder against her chest. "Sneaking up on me. I don't know how someone your size moves so quietly."

He wore no shoes. She noticed that now as he silently crossed the room on those big, bare, sexy feet. Reflexively, she backed up a step, until the edge of the desk cut across the top of her thighs and halted her progress.

"Find what you were looking for?"

"I wasn't looking for anything in particular," she replied a little too quickly. It sounded like guilt. It sounded like a lie.

He came to a halt in front of her. So close she caught the scent of citrus and bergamot and recently showered male skin on an indrawn breath. So close she could see the scepticism in the slant of his mouth and the arch of one dark eyebrow. "Not even for me?" he asked.

"Well, yes. For you."

"And here I am," he said smoothly, touching fingertips to the centre of his chest. "Not on my desk."

Warmth flooded her face, but she kept her chin high. Her eyes fixed on his, not on his chest. "I brought coffee." She gestured vaguely toward the low table, where she'd left the pot. "And I wanted to check if you'd received any more news. About your horse."

"The crisis has passed."

"She will recover?"

"God willing."

"I am glad." A relieved half smile softened the tension in her face, and Isabelle thought she saw that same emotion echo momentarily in his eyes. "Seeing your anxiety this afternoon…" Her smile gathered warmth. "That horse must be very special."

"She is, but I would have felt the same for any member of my family, equine or human."

"That, I understand."

"Do you?" he asked softly, but there was a new hardness in his expression. A deepening of the creases that fanned from the corners of his eyes as he regarded her narrowly for several heartbeats. "I have to wonder about this sentiment, this show of concern, the coffee, the sustenance. How many times would you have hauled your pretty little backside up those stairs, waiting for an opportunity to search my desk?"

Finally he'd stopped circling and pounced. So unexpectedly that Isabelle was taken aback. She drew a quick, startled breath. And discovered that she no longer wanted to run. She wanted to defend herself and her backside. "That was never my purpose," she stated emphatically.

"And yet…" He gestured at the desk behind her, his meaning obvious.

"You weren't here, so I took the opportunity to—"

"Snoop?"

"To seek answers."

Unable to bear the suspense of waiting alone downstairs for news of Gisele's fate, she'd taken every opportunity to deliver coffee and food. If there'd been any excuse to stay, to offer comfort and support, she would have jumped all over it. Her sentiment had not been fake, and she resented the implication that she'd used the situation to her advantage.

It was only on this final occasion, when she found the room empty, that she'd taken any notice of the desk and the loose pile of papers. The temptation to look for a link to the Harrington name had been too great to resist. She had no idea what she'd thought she might find.

Certainly not a glossy publication titled *Now You're Pregnant*.

"I was waiting until the crisis with your horse had passed," she said tightly, "before seeking those answers."

"Go right ahead," he invited. "Ask away."

"Why are you here?" She lifted her chin and met his gaze. "Did you really have business in Melbourne or did Hugh Harrington send you?"

His pause before answering was telling. So was the glint of acknowledgement in his eyes. When he answered with another question—"I take it you know him?"—Isabelle's composure snapped.

Whirling around, she pushed papers left and right until she found the magazine, then turned back with it brandished in her hand. "You came here at his behest to, what? Find the woman who'd called him, whose call he didn't bother to return? And what is this, your research material?" She shoved the glossy cover at his too-close chest. A vain act—that hard wall of muscle didn't budge. "Were you going to compare pictures against the real thing?"

"I needed a reference point," he said in cool, casual contrast to her heated outburst. "I had no idea what three months pregnant would look like."

"Why should that matter to you? You're not the father."

"And Hugh Harrington is?"

Isabelle's brow pulled tight. "Are you suggesting that he isn't?"

"I am asking a straight question, Isabelle. Is Harrington the father of your baby?"

"*My* baby?" The syllables exploded from her mouth husked in shock. She shook her head and couldn't hold back a short, incredulous laugh. "You think that he slept with *me*? That *I'm* pregnant?"

His incisive glare cut through her astonishment. "Are you Isabelle Browne or not?"

"Yes. I am."

"But you're not pregnant."

"No, most definitely." Isabelle expelled a harried breath and held up a hand to stop any further questions. "Let me explain. My sister Francesca—Chessie—filled in for me back in January."

"Doing this job?"

"More or less. It was supposed to be a weekend appointment, cooking for your friend in a home at Portsea. He knew the owners through business or whatever." She made a dismissive gesture; the details didn't matter, only the outcome. "They loaned him the use of their holiday place. I came down with the flu, and Chessie stepped in. She'd worked for the agency before. She's capable, but she was no longer on the books."

"So she used your name."

Isabelle nodded. If she'd not been miserably ill at the time, she would never have agreed. "It was last minute, and Chessie was available. She convinced me that I shouldn't give up the job."

"Or the money," he added dryly, but condemnation narrowed his gaze and stiffened the set of Isabelle's shoulders.

"I've already told you that money is important in my situation."

"And I believed you were referring to the additional expense of a baby."

"I was! But that is an additional expense on top of my mortgage and every other bill that must be paid."

"It's your sister's baby," he said after a moment's pause. Their eyes met and held, and for the first time she saw that he was coming around to believing her. One small step in the right direction, but an immensely important one.

"My sister's," she echoed, "and your friend's."

His gaze fell away but not before she'd seen the edge of fierceness. A word that sounded like a curse fell from his tongue as he turned and strode toward the terrace. For several seconds he stared out into the darkness before he spoke. "Hugh Harrington isn't only my friend." Slowly he turned to face her, his expression so grim and forbidding that she felt a shiver of foreboding deep in her flesh. "He is my sister's fiancé."

The shiver turned to ice-cold shock in Isabelle's belly. She remembered what he'd told her a few minutes earlier: that he would feel the same commitment, the same despair, if any member of his family was suffering. She recalled the fierce edge to his expression and knew that he'd been thinking about his sister suffering.

She knew that fierceness. She understood.

"That's why you are here," she said softly. "For your sister."

"She doesn't know. While your sister has been growing his baby, Amanda has been planning their wedding."

Isabelle had to moisten her suddenly dry mouth before she could ask, "When?"

"The thirtieth of May."

Three weeks. She swallowed. "What are we going to do about this?"

"I think it's time we brought your sister into this discussion, don't you?"

The words were so cold, his face still so uncompromisingly hard, that Isabelle's indignation blazed anew. "Don't you think you should reserve your anger for the one who deserves it?"

"Believe me, Isabelle, I have enough to go around."

Francesca Browne was the woman Cristo had expected to meet when he arrived in Melbourne.

Blond with a cover-girl face and a body to match, she bore all the trademarks of Hugh's string of girlfriends of days gone by. She arrived at Pelican Point less than ten minutes after Isabelle's phone call, wearing a stylishly loose dress that disguised any sign of pregnancy. Murmuring an apology, she hugged her sister hard before turning a level gaze on him. "So you're Mr. Fix It," she said.

"I prefer Cristo," he replied. "I doubt this is a situation I can fix."

Her perfectly shaped brows rose slightly. "You don't think you can pay me off?"

"I have no intention of attempting to," he informed her. "Would you like to come through to the living room? I can assure you it is more comfortable than standing here in the foyer."

Cristo stepped back to let the sisters go first, and they did so arm in arm, talking sotto voce as they went. He followed. He didn't try to eavesdrop. It was enough to watch them, to see their attachment, to know that this version of what happened three months ago made unfortunate sense.

Francesca Browne may well have slept with Hugh Harrington. Isabelle had not. A selfish kernel admitted that he liked this version one hell of a lot better than the alternative.

"Do you often use your sister's name?" he asked after they'd settled.

"No," Francesca replied.

"I explained why she worked under my name," Isabelle added. She'd taken a seat on the sofa beside her sister, so they presented a united front of dignity and indignation. Cristo approved of this warrior woman prepared to do battle on her sister's behalf. He respected the tigerish set to her expression and the green fire in her eyes as she went on the attack once more. "She could hardly use her own name when she called Harrington. He wouldn't have had a clue who Chessie Browne was."

"He didn't have a clue who Isabelle Browne was."

"Are you saying he doesn't remember Chessie?"

"He denies ever meeting her."

"He met me," the younger sister joined in with bitter equanimity. She touched a hand to her belly. "I hold the evidence right here."

"*You* believe us," Isabelle interceded.

She posed the words as a statement rather than a question, and when Cristo's gaze meshed with hers he felt the power of that emphatic note. He wanted to reassure her, to wipe the last shadows of uncertainty from her expression, but he was not yet in a position to do so. His instincts about this woman—about the veracity of her story—were strong but he needed to be one hundred percent certain they were no longer adversaries but united in a common cause.

"I am not the one you need to convince," he told her with an apologetic hitch of one shoulder.

"Then why are you here, if not to answer that question? You said Harrington didn't send you. You said he didn't remember meeting Chessie."

Leaning forward in his chair, he strengthened the connection of their eye contact. "He came to me for advice on how to handle Francesca's claim of paternity. I was coming to Australia on business. He did not ask me. I chose to meet you."

"By employing me under false pretences?"

"I concede that did not work out as I had anticipated. However," he added, eyes still fixed on hers, "I would do it over again for the sake of my sister's future happiness."

"The end justifies the means?"

"When it comes to my family, yes. Always."

Cristo's focus was all on Isabelle, his expression as intense as his words. But in the short silence that followed, he heard Francesca clear her throat. Saw her raise her hand in an appeal for attention.

"Hello. Would someone like to fill me in on what is going on?" Despite the blithe tone, bewilderment clouded her eyes as they shifted from Cristo to Isabelle and back again. "What does my pregnancy have to do with your sister's happiness?"

Meeting Isabelle's gaze once more, he inclined his head,

silently giving his consent for her to go ahead. Her nostrils flared as she exhaled heavily. "I'm sorry, Chess, but there's no easy way of saying this. Hugh Harrington is engaged to Cristo's sister. Their wedding is in three weeks."

Francesca's mouth rounded in a silent O of shock. She blinked and dropped a barely audible profanity. Given the circumstances, Cristo could not blame her. "Does she know about me…about the baby and the call I made to Harry?"

Cristo registered her use of the nickname. Amanda used it, along with several of their closest friends, but very few others. No other single word could have provided such convincing—or condemning—evidence. "No," he said flatly. "She doesn't."

Francesca chewed her lip a second, digesting that knowledge. "I gather you are here on your sister's behalf, to find out the truth?"

Cristo nodded.

"And now you know, what do you intend doing with it?"

"Since he maintains no knowledge of you or any relationship, there is only one solution. You and Harrington in the same room, face-to-face."

"How is that possible?" Francesca said slowly.

He turned to Isabelle, who had listened to this last exchange in stiff-backed silence. Her eyes were huge in a face as pale as her sister's. "Are your passports up-to-date?" he asked. "You are going to need them."

<u>Six</u>

Isabelle started shaking her head before he finished speaking. "We can't just up and go to England. It's impossible."

"You don't have current passports?"

"We do," Chessie supplied helpfully. "We needed them for Bali last year."

"Then what is the problem?" Cristo asked. "Is money an issue?"

"It's always an issue and even more so now."

"It doesn't have to be." Despite Chessie's responses, he spoke directly to Isabelle. "I will fly you to London. You will stay in my home. All your expenses will be covered."

His hooded gaze fixed on hers with steadfast purpose, and Isabelle felt a trill of alarm. This was a man used to taking control, to getting his way. If she didn't stand her ground, then her impulsive sister would be swept along on the tide of his will.

She straightened her shoulders. "It's not only the costs involved. I have a job."

"It is my understanding that you are engaged by me for the remainder of this week."

"You still want me?" she blurted unthinkingly.

Something flared in his eyes, a slow note of danger. "Why should I not? I have a contract for your services, one week, paid in advance."

"But you can't want a housekeeper when you're returning to England. I imagine you have staff coming out of the rafters."

"Not quite," he said smoothly, but that banked fire still smouldered in his eyes. "I prefer my staff to be more discreet."

For a long moment Isabelle floundered in the treacherous undercurrents of the exchange, in wanting and services and discretion. She needed to keep paddling to stay on top of this conversation. "You don't need a housekeeper," she repeated with more force.

"Probably not, but I am attempting to make this easy for you."

Easy? She might have laughed if this subject weren't so deadly difficult.

"You implied that your job may prevent you accompanying your sister to London," he continued, "but your job is in my employment."

"For one week."

"Which I will extend, on the same terms. Let's say an extra two weeks—" he spread his hands in a gesture of appeasement, probably because Isabelle's eyes had goggled with a combination of shock and suspicion "—to make up for any inconvenience."

"I can't do that."

"Why not? Your next job for Miriam doesn't start for weeks

yet," Chessie pointed out. Isabelle gave her a withering look. A traitor at her side was not helpful.

"Your sister raises a valid point. Why not?"

"Because you admitted that you have plenty of staff. You can't possibly need me."

"But I do." Chessie exhaled with audible impatience. "Why are you being so stubborn? Why can't you just accept Cristo's offer? It sounds enormously generous. What have you got to lose?"

Chessie spoke the words. It was Chessie's blue-green eyes that reproached hers. But in her mind's eye she saw determined onyx, heard those same words in a dark baritone, felt a shiver of alarm and mistrust and, God help her, wanton excitement.

What did she have to lose? Oh, just her pride and any semblance of control over her unruly hormones.

"We have to think this over," she cautioned. Focusing on her sister, she shut out those watchful black eyes through sheer bloody-minded willpower and lowered her voice. "Don't be steamrolled into doing what's most convenient for anyone else. Have you thought about what's best for you and the baby?"

"You know I have, and this is exactly what I would have done myself if I could have afforded the airfare."

It was true. They'd been over this territory twice before, when Chessie first learned of her pregnancy and again little more than a week ago when, with her first trimester safely behind her, she'd decided to contact the father. Isabelle hadn't been able to talk her out of making that phone call, and now she felt a fatalistic sense of déjà vu.

When had Francesca Ava Browne ever done a proper risk evaluation before plunging into the unknown? From the first time she launched herself on chubby toddler's legs she had been unstoppable—not that this had ever stopped Isabelle from trying. "That's the point," she persisted. "You *can't* afford it. What if something goes wrong? You'll be stranded on the other side of the world with no money and no support."

"And if I don't go, I will be stuck here relying on you for support you can't afford to give." When Isabelle opened her mouth to object—she had always found money for Chessie; she always would!—her baby sister held up a hand. Suddenly she looked and sounded very grown-up. Isabelle felt the sand shifting beneath her feet. "I need to do this, for me and for the baby. I'm going, Belle. Whether you do or not is up to you."

They arrived in England on Wednesday evening and were whisked to the heart of London in a chauffeur-driven car. Settling into the luxurious leather-upholstered rear seat, Chessie elbowed Isabelle for at least the hundredth time since they'd left Melbourne, mouthing "Wow!"

That enthusiasm had become old somewhere over the centre of Australia, and Isabelle used her last remaining energy to grit her teeth. She'd snapped once already, at a refuelling stop in Dubai. Chessie asked Cristo if they were staying long enough for a look around, and Isabelle, tired and anxious and edgy, had snipped, "For Pete's sake, Chessie, this is not a holiday jaunt."

"I'm well aware of what this trip is about," her sister had responded calmly, "but that doesn't mean I can't enjoy the fringe benefits."

Of course Cristo overheard the exchange, and she'd felt his silent judgement slap her right through her travel-lagged irritability. She was supposed to be the serene, sensible sister. Somewhere around her twelfth birthday, Gran had first referred to her as Capability Browne and she'd hugged that reference close, unconsciously adopting the label as the person she wanted to be. Calm, composed, capable.

But these past days—ever since Cristiano Verón had stormed into her life—she'd become someone else entirely. Angry, argumentative, anxious. She'd blamed him and his unpredictability, she'd blamed the worry of Chessie's situation, but now it was time to put on her big-girl's blouse and take responsibility.

She was here to support Chessie, to ensure that her needs weren't overlooked in deference to Cristo's sister. She needed to be alert and on her game. She needed to forget her personal disappointment over how he'd deceived her, feigning interest in her life and her family and her dreams all in the guise of uncovering "her" pregnancy.

That didn't matter now. Protecting Chessie did.

As the big sedan glided to a halt outside a row of elegant town houses, she forced herself to relax the tension in her jaw and her shoulders. And when she glanced across, she saw the same tension etched in Chessie's face. She reached—and it was quite a reach across the width of the backseat—for her sister's hand and gave it a reassuring squeeze.

Chessie's fingers gripped hers for a second. They were ice-cold, but her smile was warm. It only trembled a little around the edges. "I'm so glad you came."

Isabelle smiled back. "So am I."

From the pavement outside, Cristo's home looked like all the others in the immaculately presented rows that lined each side of Wentworth Square. Isabelle blinked in surprise at the traditional facade. She'd expected something more unique, flashy, exotic.

Then she reminded herself that this was Cristiano Verón. Mr. Unpredictable himself.

Inside, she had to remind herself several times more.

Through her job, she was used to grand homes decorated to within an inch of their stylish lives. Most had graced the pages of at least one glossy design magazine. This place transcended anything she'd seen by, oh, about a thousand percent. And, she guessed, several million pounds.

As they trailed through room after room of Georgian splendour, even Chessie was reduced to gaping, wide-eyed silence by the exquisite detail of the cornice work and the marble fireplaces and the antique furniture. Not to mention the staircase that rose through the centre of the building, with galleried landings on each of the three upper storeys. All were lined with ornately crafted railings.

And then there was their guide on this tour of the house. Cristo had introduced him simply as Crash. No further explanation as to his position in the household or whether that was his first or last name. Isabelle had wondered if perhaps he was Krasch or Craczj or some other obscure foreign spelling, until he spoke in a voice that could have played all-England. He'd relayed a series of messages to Cristo, who soon after disappeared to his rooms on the first floor, and she'd pegged him as the butler. Although his unorthodox black jeans and T-shirt, shaggy haircut and unshaven jaw belied such a tame label.

Whatever his position, he showed immense pride in the house. "Cristo bought it three years ago," he told them as he showed them to their rooms…correction, their *suite* of rooms. "Previous owner had a rubbish eye for decorating. We only finished the refit late last year."

Isabelle paused in the centre of the sitting room that separated their bedrooms. "You did the whole place out? That must have been a challenge."

"The challenge was retaining the original design elements while making it liveable."

Chessie raised her eyebrows at that description. She almost touched the floor-to-ceiling drop of voile curtaining before withdrawing her hand. "Are we allowed to touch?" she asked.

"Everything," Crash replied dryly, "except the Renoir."

"You're kidding me." Chessie peered at the painting over the fireplace, then made a strangled sound. "You're not! Far out." She whirled around. "And those pictures in the drawing room… They're originals, aren't they?"

"You want to take a closer look?"

Chessie's eyes boggled, and Isabelle waved them off. Not that she wasn't interested in art, just not as passionately engrossed as her sister. And she was keen on talking to Cristo before he left for his country estate. He'd mentioned that to Crash earlier; he had to check that his beloved horse was recovering as well as his staff had promised. But despite this impatience, he'd noticed her worried frown and invited her to track him down after she had settled in.

Crash had pointed out his rooms on the first floor, and on her way down Isabelle chewed over the notion of ever settling in at this house. Artwork by the masters hung on every wall. The thick carpet runners that muffled her footsteps were works of art in themselves.

This world of million-dollar decorating makeovers and chauffeured limousines and private jets he copiloted…this was the world of Cristiano Verón and, she imagined, Hugh Harrington.

It was a world the Browne sisters worked in, not a world they lived in.

The only way she could pretend to settle in was as a working employee—not a token one—and only after she knew when Cristo planned to approach Harrington. She'd not had a chance to broach the question since that night in Melbourne. Caught up in the logistics of packing and leaving so swiftly, then in the travel with Chessie at her side, she'd not had a minute alone with Cristo. Now she would.

Hand fisted to knock, she hesitated just long enough to pray that she'd chosen the right door. Sitting room, not bedroom. The knock-knock of her heart resonated as loudly as her knuckles on the thick timber door.

It opened immediately, as if she'd caught him on his way out. Except he couldn't be—not unless he'd chosen to go out on a chilly London evening wearing nothing but a pair of jeans and the phone pressed to his ear. Beyond the impressive breadth of his bare-skinned shoulders, beneath the thickly muscled arm with which he held the door ajar, she could see a bed.

A big, broad bed smothered in a deep chocolate spread. It looked like velvet. It looked like him.

Her gaze rocketed from the bed to his face. There was something in his hooded gaze, a glimmer of heat and of predatory satisfaction, an invitation to come into his lair and do more than talk. Suddenly she was no longer tired; she was wide awake, alive with the tingle of anticipation and the whisper of danger.

Wrong door, she reminded herself with a snap to attention. *Wrong bed, wrong tingles and absolutely the wrong man.*

Cristo was expecting her, but not this soon—he'd barely had time for a quick shower, let alone to finish dressing—and not at his bedroom door. Not that he minded. Any interruption from this phone call was welcome. When the interruption was Isabelle Browne with her hair a loose tumble of honeyed curls and her eyes wide and warm and taken aback, it was even more welcome.

"I will call you back," he said into the phone, cutting off Vivi's rant about the wedding caterer. "I have company."

His company stood on the wrong side of the threshold, shaking her head and mouthing something about coming back later. Cristo held the door wider. "Are you coming in or not?"

"Not if I'm interrupting."

"You can always help." He lifted one unclothed shoulder to indicate his meaning.

For the briefest of moments, her gaze drifted with the notion, before she snapped to attention. "I meant the phone call."

"That was only my mother," he said dismissively. Then, when her eyes widened with disapproval, he elaborated. "She wanted to discuss a problem with the wedding arrangements."

"When there may not be a wedding," she murmured, picking up on his meaning.

"Indeed."

Their gazes met in a moment of solemn accord, a reminder of what still sat between them. Her being here in his house, in his bedroom, was not about them or the fizz of physical attraction. Yet. The seriousness of the situation with Harrington and her sister lurked, dark as a thundercloud, on the horizon. But when he'd opened the door and found her standing there, when he felt the heat of her gaze taking him in and the lightning-bolt response low in his belly, he knew there would be a time for them.

He could be patient. Opening his bedroom door to a willing Isabelle would be worth the wait.

Leaving the door wide open, he retreated to an armoire and deposited the phone. In the wall mirror he saw her swallow her reservations, lift her chin and step into the room…not very far into the room, however. Barely over the threshold she paused, her unsettled gaze skating from the bed to his shirtless back and on around the room. She looked uncomfortable and out of sorts.

Because this was his bedroom, because he was only half-dressed, because she too felt the crackle of awareness and wanted to run from it. A pity this was the wrong time. He would have enjoyed the chase.

Suppressing that desire, he turned to the bed, sat and reached for his shoes and socks. "Correct me if I'm wrong, but I am assuming that you didn't come down here to watch me dress."

"Have you spoken to Harrington?" she asked quickly, but he felt the warm glide of her gaze over his shoulders and back as he bent to pull on a shoe. He glanced up and caught her looking. He saw the involuntary flare of her nostrils, the softening of her bottom lip, the guilty flush of colour in her cheeks, and gave up the fight to suppress his elemental response.

She looked at him like that, his body responded. So be it.

"Unfortunately, I haven't," he said slowly in response to her question.

Her chin came up, her gaze sharpening on his. "Why ever not?"

"Because he isn't answering his phone."

"Does he know that you found Chessie? Did you leave a message?"

"With Amanda?" he asked dryly.

"What about at work," she persisted. "Surely he has a secretary or an assistant."

"That would be Amanda."

"Oh."

Cristo watched her chew at her bottom lip while the heat stirred in his belly and thighs and all points in between. "I may not hear from him for several days," he warned, predicting her next question. "He is out of town."

"Where?"

"Does it matter?"

For a second he thought she would question that, as well, but then she let go her indignation on a weighty sigh. Her shoulders slumped and that signal of defeat, small but definite, brought Cristo to his feet.

"This is not such a bad outcome," he said. "You and Francesca can use a day to recover from the flight. Catch up on your sleep, relax, and when he does arrive you will be ready to deal with the meeting and the outcome."

She did not look convinced. Worry creased between her brows as he closed down the space between them. He had no purpose in mind other than a need to be nearer, to ease that worry, to see her eyes spark once more. Through the open door he heard voices—Crash's gruff murmur, Francesca's response. He cocked his head, drawing Isabelle's attention to the sound. "Your sister will appreciate the time to get her bearings, surely."

"You're right about Chessie," she relented. Wary eyes followed him as he passed. She jumped a little as he closed the door, isolating them from the distraction of those voices.

"And what about you, Isabelle?" he asked, turning to meet her chary gaze. He could have smiled to ease the moment. He could have backed off and allowed her more space. Instead, he leaned forward and touched a thumb to the dark circle beneath one eye. "You didn't sleep on my plane. I hope you will feel comfortable enough here to make up for that lack."

"That depends."

"On?"

Her chin came up, her eyes met his with resolute purpose. "My role in your household."

"Guest doesn't work for you?"

"Not when you are paying me, no."

Cristo folded his arms over his chest and regarded her

silently for a moment. It was a pretence. He'd known she would not let this go, that she would insist on taking up some form of paid employment. "What do you have in mind?" he asked.

"That's not for me to say when I don't know your staff arrangements. I'm not even sure of Crash's position. Is he your butler?"

"Butler, cook, valet. He runs the house."

"Alone?"

"Pretty much."

She drew a strong breath, and her eyes darkened with a new determination. "Then I'm sure he could use help. Perhaps in the kitchen."

Cristo's lips quirked.

"Is that a problem?" she asked, noticing.

"Crash is, shall we say, a little territorial."

"About his kitchen?"

"About the whole house." When questions shadowed her expression, he continued. "Crash oversaw the renovations and the decorating. He lives here. I spend more time away than under this roof."

"At your country place?"

"Chisholm Park is home, but I don't spend as much time there as I would like. My life necessitates travel." He lifted a shoulder, a gesture of acceptance of what his life entailed. "This place is a convenience when I'm in the city, and a business asset. Clients are impressed."

"I imagine so," Isabelle said, looking around the room with a new perspective. As impressive as the formal rooms and the guest suites were, she couldn't place Cristo in them. He was too big, too uncompromisingly male and too comfortable with all that masculinity. This room, however, was different. "You had a hand here," she mused. "This is you."

"Well noticed," he said.

Just two words, offered with the same insouciance as all that came before, but the flame in his eyes sucked all the air from Isabelle's lungs. Beyond the door she heard muffled voices, but still she could not look away. She could not breathe. She could not do anything to break the overwhelming intensity of the moment.

"At some point you must tell me how you reached that conclusion," he said, his voice as dark and slumberous as his eyes, "and what you see as 'me.'"

Before she could think how to answer, a knock sounded at the door. A female voice that wasn't Francesca's was raised to a level that would have reached across to the depths of the dressing room. "Cristo, your goon says you are not to be disturbed, but I think he's having a lend. If you really do have a woman in there, you'd best say so quickly because otherwise I'm coming in."

"My sister," Cristo said smoothly, eyes still fixed on Isabelle's. "Shall I tell her to go away?"

Was he serious? Was that wicked message in his eyes for real? Isabelle's heart did a funny quickstep. Her mouth opened and shut, but no sound came out.

"Cristo?" Amanda rapped loudly at the door. "I'm serious. I really do need to talk to you."

Cristo's eyes met hers, the teasing heat now overlaid with regret. "We are going to need an explanation."

"For me being here?"

"For you being here in my bedroom, yes, but more importantly, for you and Francesca being here in my house."

Seven

Amanda burst through the door in a flurry of righteous indignation. She punched Cristo's arm, then she hugged him, all the while admonishing him for not opening the door, for not answering any of her messages over the past week and finally for disappearing to Australia without any explanation.

Cristo, Isabelle noticed, did not attempt to get a word in. He pretended to wince at the puny punch, and he hugged her back with what looked like genuine affection and a large dose of forbearance that Isabelle thought was largely for show. They made quite a picture—he a big cat, all golden-skinned power, his sister a kittenish beauty with a sleek brunette bob and porcelain-pale skin.

Without drawing breath, Amanda launched from general complaints into a specific and passionate tirade about unapproved changes to the menu for her wedding breakfast. At her indignant "Harry despises shellfish. I told the planner—she doesn't listen," Isabelle's stomach twisted. She hated high melodrama—that had been her mother's specialty; it still tied her in knots of anxiety—but after a minute of observing Amanda she knew Hugh's return and Chessie's revelations would not be received with calm, levelheaded stoicism.

Feeling like an intruder on a private family moment, she'd slunk back out of view, wanting nothing more than to blend into the furniture. This wasn't impossible; it was a skill she'd learned early in life that held her in good stead in her work.

But now she longed for true invisibility because Cristo was turning his still-fuming sister beneath his arm, his intent clear. Isabelle's eyes widened with a *no, please don't!* appeal. Which he, dammit, spoke right over.

"Take a breath before you hyperventilate," he told his sister. "And after you've done that, you might say hello to Isabelle."

"Oh, I'm so sorry," Amanda said. Her pansy-dark eyes took in Isabelle with undisguised curiosity. "I didn't even notice you there. You must think I'm completely self-absorbed."

"You are," Cristo murmured.

"I know," she agreed blithely. Her smile for Isabelle held genuine warmth and a complete lack of repentance. "This wedding has turned me into an utter bridezilla. I can't wait until it's all over and I'm myself again. Or myself under the new name of Mrs. Hugh Harrington," she added.

Isabelle's heart sunk. Her eyes sought Cristo's for help, for guidance, for anything to stop this conversation descending into complete hell. He obliged by releasing his sister and reaching for Isabelle's hand. He drew her close to his side and shocked her all the way to her toes by pressing a kiss to the top of her head.

"Isabelle is the reason I flew to the other side of the world," he continued, his voice dropping to a level that made all her female bits tingle, even while her sensible, logical self shrieked an objection.

Cristo squeezed her hand in warning, and she pressed her lips shut.

Amanda had not missed a thing. Her inquisitive eyes shifted from Isabelle to Cristo. "My, my, big brother, you are full of surprises."

What could she say? The biggest surprise is still to come? She's here in this house and pregnant with your lying, cheating fiancé's baby?

What if they bumped into each other, right now, on the stairs? With both Amanda and Chessie oblivious. Sick with the thought of that confrontation, she sent a beseeching look up at Cristo.

"Crash has got it," he said casually, but there was reassurance in his expression and in the strength of his hand holding hers. Crash must have been prewarned about keeping Chessie out of the way. Isabelle did not have a problem with that. Subtly she returned the press of Cristo's palm against hers, absorbing the heat and his energy and telling herself it was okay to enjoy the sensation. It was a necessary act; for Chessie and for Amanda she could play along.

A tiny frown creased Amanda's forehead. "What has your gorilla got?"

"Kitchen emergency," Cristo replied smoothly. "Isabelle was wanting to help with dinner. I've been convincing her that help isn't necessary."

Amanda turned accusing eyes on her brother. "If you had told me you were eating in, I would have cancelled my plans and joined you."

"Perhaps that is why I didn't tell you."

"Well, I know when I'm de trop," she sniffed. "I'll leave

you to whatever you were about to get up to, but please will you speak to the caterer? He pays no attention to me or to the planner, but you have weight."

Cristo assured her that he would deal with it. With that off her shoulders, Amanda kissed them both warmly on each cheek in a very Continental manner and assured Isabelle that she would call and arrange a date "to lunch at Ivy," before departing as abruptly as she'd arrived.

A second later her face reappeared at the door.

"I almost forgot. Vivi is in Rome for an exhibition for Patrizio." She rolled the *r* in the name and her eyes simultaneously. "She left strict instructions that I was to attend the Delahunty gala, but Harry won't be back in time and now you are, so I think I can quietly opt out." Her eyes slid to Isabelle and back. "I imagine you will be taking Isabelle, which will certainly make the night…interesting."

"Good night, Amanda," Cristo said firmly, closing the door on her cheeky grin.

Isabelle had no idea what that exchange was about. Her mind spun with names but also with a heady sense of relief because so much could have gone wrong and hadn't. In the post-Amanda quiet, she could feel the textured heat of Cristo's hand more intensely. Alone that connection felt stronger, more intimate. He stood too close, their arms aligned from shoulder to wrist, his thigh a whisper away from hers. She knew she should put an end to this charade—she would, once her mind stopped spinning.

"So that was your sister," she said, because something had to be said. "She is…" Her voice trailed off because she didn't know quite how to describe the pint-size virago.

"Loud? Exhausting? Overindulged?"

"Well, it takes someone to do the indulging," she said, and

he laughed, a lazy ripple of amusement that did crazy things to her pulse.

"I accept some culpability." He shifted slightly; Isabelle felt the brush of his hip against hers. Some parts of her body melted, others tightened, but she sensed a shift in the mood along with his stance, and her whole being tuned in to that weighty tension. Despite the laughter, she knew he was about to get serious.

"Amanda was born with a heart murmur," he said. "She was always this tiny little thing, fragile but game. She's had a string of operations, but she would not give up, even when her heart stopped beating. So, yes, we tend to indulge her. We have only ourselves to blame."

Her heart had stopped beating? Little wonder he was so protective. Isabelle had never faulted him for that, but now that she knew the full story…all the physical sensations were forgotten as she grappled with a new, deeper, more dangerous desire. She wanted more than her fingers curled in his. More even than to curl into his body, to wrap her arms around him, to reach for his mouth to taste that husky male laughter.

She wanted to know more.

She wanted to know *him.*

"And now?" she asked, the emotion gruff in her voice. "She looks healthy."

"Healthy as an ox. The last operation did the trick."

"I'm glad."

And she was sincerely glad. Amanda had such vivacity about her, and she hated the thought of that spark dimmed by Hugh's perfidy. She'd liked Amanda at first sight, loathed the perfidious Hugh without meeting him. "She sounds very attached to her fiancé."

"Unfortunately, yes. She believes this is true love."

Isabelle heard the cynical edge to those last words. "And you don't?"

"I believed they were well suited," he replied. Adroitly avoiding the issue of love, Isabelle noted. "Amanda has known Hugh a long time. She's great friends with his sister and knows all the family—and she's worked for Harringtons as his PA the past two years. Yet despite all she's seen firsthand, she set out to win him."

"All what, exactly?"

"He has a reputation for partying hard. I suspect that he's more than earned the tag of Heartbreaker Hugh."

In spite of the heat of his hand holding hers, Isabelle felt a coldness inside. Heartbreaker Hugh did not sound like a man who would stand by Chessie. "Yet you seem very involved in the wedding arrangements…."

"As Amanda's brother and guardian. Don't get me wrong, Isabelle. I didn't approve of their engagement at first. It has taken Hugh a year of devotion to Amanda to win me around. I thought he'd grown up," he said darkly. "I thought this marriage might actually stand a vague chance of success."

This marriage. Isabelle turned the telling phrase over in her mind, recalling what she'd learned of his family history in the Mornington restaurant. "As opposed to your mother's two?" she asked.

"Make that four."

Four? Isabelle swallowed. "Your mother has been married four times?"

"And currently considering a fifth. Patrizio, who entertains us all with his newfound career as an artist." His lips twisted into a cynical facsimile of a smile. "Vivi believes in true love, too, you see. She just hasn't quite found one that lasts longer than the honeymoon."

There didn't seem anything to say in answer to that. As much as she appreciated his frankness and this extra insight into his family, Isabelle was left feeling hollow and dispirited. She needed something to latch on to, to lash out at, and his manipulation of her presence in his bedroom seemed the perfect target. She tugged at her hand, and he, surprisingly, let her go without argument.

"How are we going to deal with what Amanda thinks she saw here?" she asked brusquely. "She thinks we are lovers."

"By the end of tonight, half of London will think the same thing."

Isabelle's head came up. She met his eyes, no longer dark with cynicism but steady and watchful. "What do you mean?"

"Amanda talks. A lot. I imagine she'll be on at least her sixth phone call by now."

"You don't sound very concerned."

"I'm not," he said evenly. "It would seem the perfect solution."

"To?"

"The question of why you and your sister flew into England on my private jet and now are ensconced in my house."

For a long moment, she stared back at him. Her heart was beating all over the shop. Was he serious? He looked serious. She puffed out a breath and shook her head. "No one will believe that you and I are lovers."

"Why not?"

"Because…look at me." Head high, she lifted her arms to indicate her ordinary looks, her plain clothes, her girl-next-door appearance, and Cristo did as instructed. He looked at her, slowly, thoroughly, intently. Hot from the inside out, she lowered her arms. "No one will believe us as a couple."

"Amanda didn't appear to have any difficulty."

"She doesn't know that I'm a housekeeper. You fly around

in a private jet. You live in Belgravia and play polo and do lunch at places I've never heard of. You do not date domestics!"

"You know this…how?"

He was being deliberately difficult. She had to make him see reason before he did something truly ludicrous, such as accepting Amanda's suggestion of taking her to this gala do. She sucked in a breath. "This function Amanda mentioned…"

"It's a charity dinner and auction," he explained, "for one of my stepfather's closest friends, who happens to be on the board of Chisholm Air. Alistair was a patron of the Delahunty Foundation. His company remains a major sponsor and supporter."

"Well, I couldn't go with you to something like that. I wouldn't know what to say or how to act. I'd be like Julia Roberts with the snails in *Pretty Woman*."

"I believe this year's theme is Russian. I'm almost certain snails will not be on the menu."

"That is not the point," she said through her teeth. She felt like grabbing him by the throat and shaking him. "I don't even have any clothes suitable for a formal function."

"A valid point," he mused after a moment's narrow-eyed consideration. Isabelle felt like breaking into the "Hallelujah Chorus." Finally he was taking this seriously. "I have to go to the office in the morning, but as soon as I can get away I will pick you up. Somewhere around one, I imagine."

The chorus in Isabelle's head stuttered to a confused halt. "Pick me up for…?"

"I'm taking you shopping," he said. "For whatever you need for this role."

"This role?" she echoed.

"As my lover, my girlfriend, my mistress, my woman. Which would you prefer?"

Isabelle went hot, then cold. It wasn't only the words he used, it was the tone. It was the dark flare of satisfaction in his eyes. It was the wicked notion tingling through her blood that perhaps he meant this to be real. "No." She shook her head adamantly. "I won't do it. I would rather scrub floors."

"Pity, because I am not in need of a charlady. You came here tonight to ascertain your role as my employee." Suddenly his expression was decisive, his demeanour all brook-no-argument business. "I do not need household help of any variety. I do not need a driver or a personal shopper or a valet." As if to reinforce that point, he crossed to his dressing room and emerged pulling on a shirt. "I need you here with your sister. I need you to keep Amanda's persistent curiosity satisfied and to run interference if her path should cross Francesca's. Do you understand?"

Isabelle's eyes rocketed from shirt buttons to his face. She nodded. This was better; this even sounded like a sensible idea. "Yes," she said with new enthusiasm. "I can do that."

"I have every confidence that you can."

"And what about the other role?"

"As my lover?"

"Your *pretend* lover." That had to be made clear right from the start.

And when he closed down the space between them, she held her ground and held his gaze. She didn't allow herself to be distracted by his hands tucking in the shirt or by the churn of heat in her blood as he stopped in front of her. "I have every confidence in you, Isabelle," he said, but there was a hint of wickedness in both voice and eyes as they drifted over her face. "I believe you will satisfy me in any role you take on, whether pretend or otherwise."

* * *

"He's paying you to be his mistress for a week? And buying you clothes?" Chessie grinned widely. "Hello, *Pretty Woman!*"

Isabelle did not grin back. She prowled the sitting room, unable to sit still. Unable to believe that she'd agreed to this ridiculous ruse or that she'd slept for twelve long hours after accepting the role. Cristiano Verón's pretend lover. In the clear light of a perfect spring morning, that idea made as much sense as her sister's movie reference.

"I'm not playing his mistress or dressing to impress his business associates. He's buying me an outfit so I don't look out of place at a charity dinner." She exhaled a soft gust of annoyance. "As if dressing me in expensive clothes will make a difference."

"Meaning what?"

"Meaning everyone will know I'm a fraud."

"Because you don't know which glass for red and which for white? Or which silverware to use for which course? Or how to unfold your serviette?" Chessie asked. "You can cook, plate and serve a formal seven-course dinner with your eyes closed, and you know it. What is the real problem? Is it Cristo?"

"It's Cristo, and it was meeting Amanda." Her gaze met her sister's and then slid away. She'd shared the gist of that meeting but not all the details. Chessie did not need the health issues influencing her decisions; that had to be between her and Harrington. "He expects me to play the part of his lover," she continued in a rush. "I know it's just acting, and an explanation for why we're here and to allay Amanda's curiosity, but he's paying me and now he's spending more money on fancy clothes."

"Necessary clothes," Chessie insisted. "Think of it as a uniform."

"A designer uniform that costs hundreds and hundreds of pounds?"

"Thousands, I imagine," Chessie said cheerfully. Then, when she saw the horror in Isabelle's eyes, "Come on, Belle, you know how these millionaires drop money. Look around you. How much would this room alone have cost to decorate? To Cristo an outfit that costs a thousand pounds would be like you dropping a five-cent coin. Why can't you just embrace it, have some fun? Like Cinderella, getting to go to the ball."

Isabelle gave her a look.

"You know what I think," her sister said thoughtfully. Wearing jeans and a sloppy joe, she still managed to look perfectly at home stretched out on an ornate cream and gold chaise longue that probably cost more than Isabelle's entire home full of furniture. "I think Cristo gets a thrill out of winding you up. I bet he's banking on more resistance. He's probably kicking back in his office right now with that wicked little smile he gets…you know the one…where just the corners of his mouth lift up?"

Isabelle swallowed. She knew that smile. It was a bone-melting mixture of rich treacle and pure testosterone. "And what do you suppose he's smiling about?" she asked her sister, intrigued despite herself.

"The prospect of another head-to-head with you. Imagine his surprise if you're waiting at the door, the ever-efficient employee, all ready to sweetly do your boss's bidding."

She could do this. Not because she subscribed to Chessie's suggestion of a game of one-upmanship—she was pretty sure that Cristo the grand master, with black belt, would have her on the figurative mat before the end of round one—but because Isabelle Browne was, at heart, an agreeable person.

After years of blocking her ears against the emotional melodramas played out between her parents, she preferred peaceable.

And no matter how aggravating she found this situation, Cristo was her boss. She had agreed to his terms; she was contracted as his employee. If a little part of her was wildly attracted to the notion of setting him off-kilter with unexpected compliance, who was to know?

She'd apprised Chessie in no uncertain terms that she wasn't playing games. That she took every one of Cristo's incendiary remarks with a grain of he-is-so-full-of-it salt. Ignoring Chessie's raised eyebrows and murmured "Methinks the lady doth protest too much," she set about locating her least-shabby jeans and underwear for the shopping expedition.

She'd narrowed the selection to a matched set of lace-trimmed lilac—a birthday gift from Chessie two years back and showing signs of age—and a basic white combination, plain but near new, when Chessie called her to the phone.

"Cristo," she said. "I can barely hear him, but I imagine he wants you."

Through the pitchy whine of jet engines, she could hear him clearly enough to recognise the all-about-business tone. He had to fly to Spain, urgent, unavoidable.

Isabelle didn't have time to summon any sense of relief before he told her he would be home for tonight's dinner. Amanda would be taking her shopping. She frowned through a ridiculous jolt of disappointment. "Isn't that a bit risky? I thought you'd be trying to keep us apart."

"Impossible. She called this morning wanting to meet us for lunch."

"Oh."

"Let her do all the talking," he advised, "and you'll be fine."

"But what about Chessie?"

"Crash will look after her."

Which is how she found herself crawling through thick London traffic in the backseat of the same chauffeur-driven car as yesterday—a Maybach, Amanda informed her, with doesn't-everyone-travel-like-this nonchalance. She'd tried to get out of the shopping trip, first when Amanda called to set a pick-up time and then when she arrived an apologetic fifty minutes late.

"Last-minute crisis," she'd explained. "Bloody job."

"You should have called me," Isabelle said, appalled that she'd dragged her away from work. "You don't have to do this."

"Oh, yes. I do." She shepherded a reluctant Isabelle out the door and toward the limo. "A couple of phone calls, problem sorted, crisis averted," Amanda continued. "Now I'm taking an extra-long lunch because I can. I have an in with the boss," she confided, wriggling her fingers so the antique-set diamond on her left hand caught the sun.

Isabelle couldn't *not* comment. "Your ring, it's stunning," she said, each word tasting thick and dry in her mouth.

"Isn't it? Harry found it at an estate sale in Bavaria."

"I suppose he travels a lot with his work."

"A lot and often. Usually I don't mind, but at the moment, with so much to do for the wedding…" Her voice trailed off, and for the briefest moment she looked exposed, almost forlorn. Then she inhaled through her nose and shot Isabelle a rueful smile. "I suspect he volunteered for this trip. 'Please, Justin, find me somewhere to go, anything to get me out of town.' This wedding has become a monster that's taken over my life."

That honesty, the deprecating humour—Isabelle was beginning to like Cristo's sister a little too much to continue the secretive charade. "Look," she said, barely able to meet her eyes. "You are much too busy for this."

"For helping Cristo out? Never. Do you know how often he's asked for my help?" Amanda raised her eyebrows, waiting for an answer.

"Um…not often?" Isabelle guessed.

"Exactly, and I want to redress the balance, just a little." Her gaze remained appealingly earnest, despite her carefree tone. "Besides, we're talking about shopping, which is one of my favourite pastimes, and spending Cristo's money. Which, according to him, is my other."

Isabelle looked dubious.

"Humour me," Amanda continued. "I've called ahead. It's all arranged. Nina is giving us private access to her whole collection."

"Nina?"

"We're here!" Amanda indicated an understated shopfront in a street of understated shopfronts.

Isabelle blinked. She had been expecting… To be honest, she didn't know. Perhaps Selfridges or Harvey Nichols or a sign that proclaimed Outrageously Expensive Couture.

"If I'd had more notice, I would have called in a stylist, but Nina is the next best thing. She has all the labels and exquisite taste. Come on," Amanda said, looping her arm through Isabelle's and gently urging her across the mile-wide seat toward the door. "Let's go spend an insane amount of my brother's money." Seeing the look on Isabelle's face, she smiled wickedly. "Don't worry, he has plenty. And when he gets an eyeful of you in full Nina-fied splendour, he won't mind a bit."

Eight

Cristo paused outside her door. The music playing inside was loud enough to recognise as Vivaldi even through the closed door. In all likelihood it would drown out the sound of his knock, but he allowed her a minute to answer regardless. According to Crash, whom he'd passed on the stairs, she was ready and waiting. According to Amanda's *mission-accomplished* text, she had the perfect dress, shoes, hairstyle.

Frankly, he'd expected more resistance. To the shopping expedition and to attending tonight's gala on his arm. Driving in from the airport, he'd thought about the upcoming clash of words and wills with much expectation and some impatience. The twenty-four hours since he'd last seen her seemed infinitely longer, and he'd stretched it another thirty minutes to shower, shave and dress. Dinner suit, black tie, standard for these events he was compelled to attend.

Tonight was different. For once he didn't feel compelled.

His body hummed with anticipation as he knocked once again. Then, done with waiting, he opened the door.

The sitting room was filled with the music's liquid notes and all the signs of a successful shopping expedition. Carrier bags, several pairs of abandoned shoes, a jewelled evening bag that caught the chandelier's sparkle and flung the light in a score of new directions.

But no Isabelle.

The door to her bedroom lay open, and through the concerto's diminuendo he caught the sparkling notes of laughter. A smile twitched at the corners of his mouth, and his body quickened with recognition. It was her voice that caused both reactions, although Francesca's was there in the background, no doubt spurring the laughter as she so often did.

Scooping up a discarded shoe from his path, he started across the room only to come to a stonewall halt when Isabelle hurried into view. Her head was turned as she flung a last comment back at her sister, and she didn't see him for several thick heartbeats. It was enough time for him to take in the picture—and, *Dios,* what a picture she made—and to pick his jaw up from the floor.

She turned, the laughter still in her eyes even as it died on her lips. She stopped. Blinked once. "You're here."

"So it would appear," he said.

The first impact had been all about her—the expanse of creamy skin, the ripple of her hair as she turned, the stimulating stroke of her laughter.

Now he took stock of the rest with a long, leisurely appraisal. Her dress, a column of scarlet. The fabric, soft and lustrous, cut and draped to make the most of her sensational figure. The rise of her breasts as she drew a breath, the shadow of cleavage that disappeared from view as she lifted a hand to the low-cut neckline.

At the other end the dress pooled over her feet to the carpet. Not quite ready and waiting. He held up the shoe in his hand. "Yours?"

"Yours," she replied, not echoing his question but answering it. The proud set of her chin let him know her meaning. She wasn't accepting his purchases. They would be worn; they would remain his property.

Their gazes met and held, a current of energy arcing between them. A new edge sharpened Cristo's anticipation. A knowledge that despite her stance and her words, she felt the same crackle of awareness. The same charged heat in her blood.

This was the Isabelle whose company he relished. The one who stood her ground, who met his gaze with steady strength to state her case.

Eyes locked on hers, he slowly closed the space between them. "If this is mine," he said, holding the delicate silvery straps in one hand and tapping the spiked heel against the palm of his other, "then do I get to put it on your foot, Cinderbella?"

At his play on her name, irritation flashed in her eyes. But before she could voice her objection, Francesca appeared in the doorway.

"Cheating," she said shortly, indicating the shoe with a wave of her hand. "Obviously that will be a perfect fit, given you bought it for her."

"Spoilsport."

"Not really," Francesca said. "Since I'm about to leave you to whatever sport you have in mind."

That earned an appreciative grin from Cristo and a cutting glare from her sister. "There's no need," she said briskly. "Once I put on the shoes, we'll be leaving, too."

"Then I will see you downstairs," Francesca replied. "I'm off to check out the coach and horses."

The door closed with a hollow thud, shutting them off. Alone. Their eyes met briefly as he handed her the shoe. "No coach," he told her. "Just the Maybach."

"Chessie likes to wind me up."

"Is Cinderella a hot button?" he asked.

"A warm one," she said, collecting the second shoe before sliding them both onto her feet. Three inches taller, she straightened and met his eyes. "Given my job, it's an old joke. Usually I pay it no mind."

"You think that tonight there is a reason to pay it mind?"

"The shopping, this dress, it's all a bit much."

"No, the dress is not too much," he countered softly. "In fact, it is precisely as I requested."

Her gaze sharpened on his, a frown tugging her newly shaped eyebrows together. "You gave Amanda specific instructions on how to dress me?"

Cristo hitched a shoulder. "General rather than specific."

"Such as?"

"I requested a dress that would enhance your beauty, not overwhelm it. This—" his voice dropped with his gaze, taking in the flutter of pulse at the base of her throat and the rosy flush in her exposed skin "—is almost perfect."

"Almost?" She stared at him, her expression a perfect blend of confusion and indignation. "The price you paid, there should not be anything lacking!"

"Just this one thing."

With a deft hand he fished a necklace from his inside pocket. Three rows of pearls fashioned into a contemporary choker, the piece was classic, simple perfection. Perfect for the dress, perfect for Isabelle.

"No." Her hand came up to her throat in a protective

gesture as she took a step back. "I told Amanda, the dress is enough. I don't need any jewellery."

"So she said, but I disagree."

"It's too much."

"Let me be the judge," he said, taking back the space she'd put between them and a little more. "Turn around," he said softly.

For a wilful second she stood her ground, shoulders squared, gaze fixed steadily on his. "Jewellery was not in the deal."

"Nor, as I recall, was hair or makeup."

Her eyes widened slightly. "If you object—"

"No, I approve."

"Good," she said darkly. "You paid enough for those, as well."

"Good," he retorted, smothering a smile. "I hope you gained some measure of enjoyment at my expense."

"You could have saved yourself a lot of money by sending me and Chessie."

"Would you have gone?" he asked, circling around her, taking in the dress from all angles. "And would you have chosen *this* dress?"

"No, there was this smoky grey one with—"

"I hate grey."

"I know."

Cristo laughed, and her frown darkened. "If you mean to annoy me, you will have to do better than that," he said softly. "I am in far too accommodating a mood."

"Your meeting in Spain, did that go well?"

That emergency seemed a lifetime ago. He'd solved it. He'd moved on. Now he wanted to concentrate on her. "Better than expected," he said, turning his focus to the tense set of her shoulders and the tumble of honey-gold hair that, although newly cut, still hit her shoulder blades. He gathered the glossy curls in one hand, baring her nape, releasing a subtle fragrance from hair and skin.

He hoped he'd wiped Spain and business from both their minds, but just in case he leaned forward to inhale the scent of warm honey and nectarine blossom and female skin. "Nice," he murmured.

"It's Jo Malone," she said faintly. "Amanda insisted."

"I must remember to thank her."

He pushed her hair forward over one shoulder and took his time sliding the pearls around her throat, absorbing the lightning spark of contact as his fingers brushed her skin. He may have imagined her quicksilver shiver of response. He did not imagine the heat rushing south in his blood.

The necklace clasp was a kindergarten task. Cristo could have managed it in the dark at any other time, but not on Isabelle's neck. His fingers preferred to linger on her skin, his gaze on the vulnerable curve beneath her ear. The temptation to lean forward, to press a kiss to that precise spot, sang with the violins in the air.

"We will never get there at this rate," she murmured, but the breathy catch in her voice was not impatience. And it spoke straight to his gathering arousal. "Let me get it."

"I wish," he murmured gruffly. Then, when she squirmed beneath his hands, "Hold still."

The catch clicked shut, but the temptation remained. He leaned close, pressed open lips to silky skin, and she leaped forward as if stung. Her hair whipped around her shoulders as she turned, but when her gaze fastened on his, something palpable churned between them. Awareness, knowledge, desire.

Her nostrils flared slightly, and whatever admonishment she'd been about to lay on him froze on her parted lips. One hand lifted, fingertips to the pearls. "Thank you," was all she said.

"My pleasure."

Cristo could have pursued the mood, could have pushed the energy swirling like the lush orchestral notes between them, but they were already late. The whole evening stretched ahead, a feast of Isabelle, a smorgasbord of opportunity.

"Ready?"

She nodded and gathered her bag. Then her gaze caught the time on the mantel clock, and the frown rushed back full tilt. "Will we be very late?" she fretted.

"Fashionably. Which could work for the better," he mused with a lazy smile.

"How is that?"

"We will be noticed, tongues will wag," he replied, taking her hand. "Arriving together, hand in hand, your hair slightly dishevelled. That should address any concerns about the credibility of our relationship, don't you think?"

Isabelle assumed he'd taken her hand as a demonstration of his point, but coming down the stairs she needed his hold for balance. She'd never worn heels so high. Amanda had dismissed her qualms. "It's a dinner," she'd said. "You'll be sitting." Nina agreed. Neither of them mentioned the perilous walking involved in getting to said dinner table, and she'd been having too much fun trying on clothes and soaking up every glimpse of Cristo offered through his sister's eyes. Amanda, as he'd said, liked to talk.

Inside the limo he took her hand again, which meant that despite the roomy interior—honestly, they could have held a charity fundraiser in the rear of this car—he was sitting far too close. Not quite touching, except when he leaned forward to point out one of the attractions beyond her side window. She leaned closer to the cool glass, peering out with feigned interest, although the passing sights barely registered.

Apparently Cristo Verón was the only attraction London had to offer her single-tracked senses.

Although understandable—handsome at the best of times, in black tie the man was truly a traffic stopper—it was an irritation that worried at her like a snappy terrier. Before and after the fact, she hated the extravagance of this afternoon's shopping, and yet at the time, she'd slipped into whatever the redoubtable Nina had passed her way. She'd walked out of the store with a staggering array of clothing, not only for tonight but to cover any likely outing over the next days.

Due to the efforts of Amanda and Nina and Perri the hair magician, she looked the part of a rich man's date, but that was only the external. What about the rest? What did Cristo expect of her at the charity gala? Would he continue to hold her hand, would they dance, would he whisper in her ear and kiss that sweet spot he'd hit upstairs?

Would that be their role, as new lovers unable to keep their hands from each other?

Heat rippled through her blood, the same sensation as when his fingertips had brushed her nape as he'd fastened the necklace. The same as every time he touched her.

Isabelle rubbed her arm in a vain attempt to dispel the tingle.

"Cold?" he asked.

"No." Far from it. "Just…nervous."

"There is no need."

"Even though we will be noticed and tongues will wag?"

His grip on her hand tightened, enough to draw her gaze around to meet his. Dark as the night, steady, serious. "I was teasing, Isabelle. There is no need for nerves. You will manage beautifully."

"You don't know me well enough to make that call. I might have appalling table manners. I might drink excessively and tell hideous jokes. I might trip over in these heels and land face-first in some duke's lap!"

"Lucky duke," he murmured, and Isabelle exhaled on a note that was part laughter and part disbelief. The awful thing? She could imagine him handling that situation with his usual sangfroid. As for her own sangfroid… Well, it hummed along with the rest of her over the compliment he was paying her with his confidence.

He'd trusted her to an afternoon with Amanda. He trusted her to play the part of his date. If she kept on remembering that—*this is a job, Isabelle, not Cinderella on her way to the ball*—then she might just get through the night.

"It would help if I knew more about this function," she said, forcing herself to concentrate on the job.

"What do you need to know? There will be an endless production of dinner courses. Some may even be edible. In keeping with the Russian theme, the entertainment may include ballet, although Cossacks on horseback are not out of the question. There will be an auction to benefit the Remember Rani Foundation, for cancer research. We will be seated at David's table."

Isabelle frowned. Names had flown at her from all directions these past few days, but that was one she did not recall. "Is David your stepfather's friend?"

"Yes. David Delahunty."

"Is there a Mrs. Delahunty?"

"The foundation is named for his late wife, Rani. He hasn't remarried." He paused, a brief beat of time, before adding, "His daughter will be there, and Rani's sister and her husband."

"What are their names?"

Isabelle prepared herself for taking mental notes, but Cristo lifted their linked hands and kissed her knuckles. "Relax, sweetheart, you are not expected to know any of these people. We have known each other for less than a week. Let's assume we haven't spent that time discussing London society."

His meaning shimmered a moment in the silence, replete with pillow-talk images. She felt the bloom of heat in her skin, but she held his gaze. For the sake of tonight's role-play, she needed to know what they'd spent the past week doing. "If we're going to pass muster as a couple," she said steadily, "then we will need a believable story."

"I suggest we stick as closely as possible to the truth."

"So, we met last week when you came to Australia on business?"

"You were my housekeeper," he continued. "The fascination was instant."

"The fascination, yes," she agreed, falling into the fiction and into the dark heat of his heavy-lidded gaze. "But I was your employee. I would lose my job if I slept with you."

"Which is why I convinced you to accompany me back to England."

"To get me into bed? Would you do that?"

The pad of his thumb traced the delicate skin at her wrist, and heat exploded low in her belly as he answered with one sure word. "Undoubtedly."

"And now we are lovers?"

"Is that a role you are willing to play?" he asked, his voice as dark and heavy as the heat in her blood.

For a long moment their gazes held, the atmosphere ripe with erotic speculation. Isabelle's heart thundered, too loud to hear her whispery caution. *It's a story, Isabelle. The role you are playing.* She moistened her lips. "Would anyone believe that we weren't?"

"Not for a second."

"This is a regular happening, then?" Her chin came up a notch to counter a silly pang of disappointment. Ridiculous, she knew, and yet she couldn't help herself. "You go away on a business trip and bring home a random woman?"

"Never random. I am very selective. Do you need details, statistics, my latest health check?"

"No," she countered quickly. "I just needed to know how I would be viewed. I have never been in this situation."

"Take your cues from me. Don't drink too much wine, leave the dukes alone, and you will do fine." His thumb traced the reverse path across her wrist. Then he nodded toward the window at her back as the car slowed and stopped. They had arrived. "Are you ready?"

There was comforting strength in his easy confidence, and Isabelle nodded. "As long as I don't forget myself and start bussing tables or—" a sudden thought widened her eyes "—I don't run into someone I've worked for!"

"Will they recognise you out of uniform?"

A good point. "You're right. They wouldn't."

Then the car door swung open to reveal a bevy of doormen in stunning livery and the pinkened glow of lamplight on flagstones and people...so many beautiful couples in dazzling evening dress and jewels—oh Lord, was that woman wearing a tiara?—and all as fashionably late as Isabelle and Cristo.

As she slid from seat to ground, Isabelle's stomach jived with nerves. She tried not to gawp but the beauty alighting from the next car looked awfully like the cover girl on the glossy magazine that graced her bedside table. "Is that Lily whatshername, the model?"

"Probably," Cristo drawled, all I-see-supermodels-every-day insouciance. His gaze barely shifted from hers as he took her hand and drew her close to his side.

To disguise her shiver of response, Isabelle turned into his body and inclined her head at the latest arrivals. "The man she's with, is that…" Her voice trailed off as her eyes widened in disbelief. "Oh my God, it is!"

"If that is Lily Whatshername, then I dare say it is." A smile kicked at his lips. "Would you like to meet them?"

"You know them? Really? No, you're winding me up!"

He laughed, a low, smoky sound that dappled her senses with shadowy heat. "I sold him a G5 last month. We're on speaking terms, although…" Taking her other hand, he pulled her closer still. Suddenly all her senses were attuned to him, this man, the slightly roughened texture of his fingers wrapped around hers, the brush of his jacket against her hip, the enveloping heat of his body. The double-shot potency of espresso eyes and voice. "I would rather you kept that sloe-eyed wonder focussed on me."

"I would," she said, "if I knew what that meant."

"It means we're playing besotted lovers, remember?"

"I haven't forgotten."

"Good." Although a smile still lurked around the corners of his mouth, the mood had turned oddly serious. Supermodels, pop stars, royalty in tiaras, the drift of orchestral music, all faded to dusk. And when he ran his hands up her arms to cup her shoulders, Isabelle couldn't do a thing to blunt her response. A tremor coursed through her, a powerful mix of hot and cold intensity that tightened her breasts and softened her belly.

For the barest of moments his gaze lifted from hers, long enough to break the hot spell of connection, enough to let in the muted chords of Russian music and German engines and posh English voices. When his eyes returned to hers, she saw the flare of intent and her heart tripped wildly as his mouth started its smooth descent. Stretching on tiptoes, she met his kiss with softened lips, breathing the citrus and bergamot on his skin, absorbing his dark male heat and spinning with the intensity of desire that swelled to fill her senses.

This is not a game, she thought. *This is absolutely real.*

But just as she ached to deepen the connection, his mouth was gone, hers left wanting more. In the time it took to regain her breath and gather her equilibrium, Isabelle felt the chill night air encroaching into her sensual cocoon. A second later she realised they were no longer alone. And as Cristo drew her around to perform the introductions to David Delahunty and his family, she realised that the chill dancing up her spine had nothing to do with the cool May night.

It had everything to do with the resentment radiating from the daughter's glacial blue eyes as they took in Isabelle's well-kissed lips.

Nine

"Did you enjoy yourself, Isabelle?"

As the limo pulled away from the kerb and commenced the return drive to Wentworth Square, Isabelle slipped out of her ill-conceived choice of shoes and pretended interest in massaging the ache from her feet. That gave her time to consider Cristo's tricky question and an excuse not to consider him. She knew he'd settled on the opposite side of the big car, that he'd loosened his bow tie, that he lounged at apparent ease as he waited on her response.

She *had* enjoyed the interesting menu and the superb champagne, the music and dancing and surreptitious celebrity-spotting. Although wide-eyed and quietly appalled at the extravagance, she'd enjoyed perusing the jewellery and art, the five-star travel and out-of-this-world experiences offered for auction. She would have enjoyed everything a whole lot more if she'd not been stewing over that kiss.

Why hadn't she realised that it was part of a carefully orchestrated show? A setup staged for Madeleine Delahunty's benefit.

On the heels of that stunner had come a second awful realisation. Despite all the self-talk about doing her job and playing a role, somewhere deep inside she had still harboured a kernel of Cinderella-going-to-the-ball hope. She'd believed in the crackling sexual energy when Cristo looked at her a certain way, when he held her hand, when he laughed low and smoky at something she said.

She'd believed in the possibility of a fairy tale, and she'd set herself up for the most crushing of letdowns.

Dumb, dumb, dumb.

And the dumbest thing of all? Her reaction. Standing there on the pavement with hot and cold chills of disappointment and mortification churning through her, she'd decided that the only suitable recourse was to play him at his own game. She'd cozied in even closer, she'd possibly even simpered and batted her eyelashes, and she'd thrown herself with uncharacteristic vengeance into the role of besotted can't-keep-my-hands-off-him lover.

Had she gone too far? Possibly. Probably. But, dammit, she wasn't going to apologise or back down now they were alone. He'd started it with that kiss. He'd invited her to follow his lead. If he didn't like how she'd followed—if *that* was the undercurrent she detected beneath the measured delivery of his question—then tough.

Setting her expression with her best attempt at cool, calm confidence, she turned to face him. "I enjoyed myself well enough, thank you."

"Perhaps a little too much."

"Did I overdo it?" she asked disingenuously. "This was my first appearance as a make-believe mistress. I wasn't sure of the boundaries, so I did as you asked and followed your lead.

I'm pretty sure that we established ourselves as a couple. That is what you wanted…?"

"I didn't know you were such an accomplished actress," he murmured darkly.

"Why, thank you. My mother would be pleased that all those drama lessons paid off."

His corner of the car rode in shadowed darkness, and she couldn't see his face clearly enough to judge his mood, but she sensed she'd surprised him. She wished that didn't please her quite so much. "So it was all an act?" His voice, too, was a tricky mix of shadow and dark. Hard to judge, hard to pick. "The way you never left my side, the little touches, your hand on my thigh."

"An act…and payback."

"For?"

"For putting me in that situation. For not telling me the whole story. For kissing me in front of your friends."

The car slowed at an intersection, and the fractured streetlight caught his face, revealing his expression for the first time. The slant of his prominent cheekbones, the shadowed planes beneath, the darkening of beard along his jawline. The softened fullness of his mouth hovering close to a smile as he drawled, "Here I was thinking, *She's taken me at my word. She's trying harder to get under my skin.*"

He was enjoying this. Isabelle couldn't believe it. Her own jaw tightened with indignation. "I was trying to irritate you!"

He laughed, a rich rumble of sound that coiled around her in sexy loops and pulled tight. "Why does that not surprise me?"

"Does anything surprise you?" she snapped.

Although they had moved on and his expression was again hidden in shadow, Isabelle sensed a shift in mood. She knew the smile was gone. Her heart beat a little harder, a lot quicker.

"You do, Isabelle," he said, soft, serious. One arm stretched across the backseat, his knuckles grazed the bare skin at her shoulder and suddenly the vast space shrunk, all the air sucked up in that one slice of a second. "Constantly."

She frowned hard, fighting his insidious charm and the expectant leap of her hormones. With a handful of words and one featherlight touch, he'd managed to turn her outrage inside out. She would not have that. She would not let him get away with such a cheap and obvious distraction. "Is that because I've shown such remarkable restraint, going along with every one of your manipulative plans when—"

"Manipulative?" he cut in, still sounding far too unrattled for Isabelle's liking. "How so?"

Turning in her seat, she fastened him with an incredulous glare. "*Everything* in the past week fits under that umbrella. The way you employed me with the sole aim of working the truth about Hugh from me, without any hint of what you were about. The way you used my concern for Chessie and my need of paid employment to coerce me into coming to England and then into playing this role of your lover. I should have known you had an ulterior motive."

"And if I had told you that my ulterior motive was getting to know you, would you have agreed to continue as my employee? Would you be here with me now?"

Getting to know her? Isabelle's heartbeat stuttered. *No.* She'd enjoyed the very fine champagne but not enough to succumb to his smooth talk. Her frown deepened to a borderline scowl. "I was talking about how you used me and our 'relationship'—" she drew the word out, each syllable served with a heavy dash of sarcasm and a side of fully justified pique "—to deliver a we're-through message to your last girlfriend."

"Are you referring to Madeleine?" He sounded surprised, unsure. As if he didn't know. As if he needed to think it over. As if!

"Unless there were other exes that I missed the pleasure of meeting tonight, then, yes, Madeleine."

"Is that what she told you? That she is my ex-girlfriend?"

"Not in so many words, but that is the message she delivered." With every barbed word, with every murderous look. "I felt the daggers in my back. Would you care to check for wounds?"

His breath checked, as if that answer had amused him again. "Later," he promised. Then, when Isabelle's glare darkened, "Do not believe everything Madeleine tells you."

"Are you telling me she's not an ex?"

"Neither girlfriend nor lover."

He'd leaned forward to capture her gaze, and despite the deception of the shadows she could not ignore the sincerity in his voice or eyes. *Damn him.* "Then her possessiveness is…?"

"A misunderstanding."

Isabelle puffed out a breath full of scepticism. "She misunderstood your interest in her? You're really 'just good friends'?"

"Exactly. I've known her from the weekend I arrived in England. David and Rani and Madeleine were the first to welcome me. Our parents were the closest of friends. We spent a lot of time together growing up. Our parents jested about us as a couple." He paused, raked a hand through his hair, and despite the matter-of-fact delivery Isabelle realised that he was uncomfortable with the subject. "My mother has, unfortunately, not given up on the joke."

"She wants to arrange your marriage?"

"Exactly," he said darkly. "In spite of her track record, Vivi believes everyone should be married."

Obviously *he* didn't. Isabelle remembered their conversation about Amanda's engagement and his cynical comments on true love. She also remembered Madeleine's cutting verbal skills—the woman's blood might run cold with venom, but her mind was as sharp as her tongue. "Surely Madeleine couldn't believe that possible, not without some encouragement from you."

"After her mother died…" He shook his head, expelled a harsh breath. "David took it hard. Madeleine needed a friend."

And Cristo was that friend, the old family connection. He'd already spoken and demonstrated his desire to do whatever was needed for his extended family. "She got the wrong idea," Isabelle said slowly, "about your interest."

"Madeleine has always been headstrong and overindulged."

Isabelle thought of a few more pertinent adjectives, but she didn't voice them. Already she had pieced together a picture she understood. Cristo at his kindest would be devastatingly hard to resist. How could she fault Madeleine for wanting him? "She is used to having whatever she wants, and now she wants you."

"Something like that."

In the lee of this exchange, Isabelle felt deflated and incredibly vulnerable. She hadn't needed this extra insight into Cristo's compassionate side—she was struggling enough with the powerful physical attraction—and now she felt unexpected sympathy for Madeleine and a degree of shame for her actions. This event was named in Rani Delahunty's honour. The charity raised funds for the cancer that had claimed her life. It would have been a difficult night for Madeleine without having Cristo's supposed new girlfriend flaunted in her face.

"So you took me along tonight," she stated tightly, "to show Madeleine what she couldn't have. Don't you think it would have been kinder to tell her straight out that you're just not that into her?"

"I have done so, many times, in many ways, but not tonight. I took you," he said with the same quiet intensity, "because I wanted to."

"Not to keep Madeleine at bay?"

"I've been keeping her at bay, as you put it, for half of my life. I do not need you for that, Isabelle."

"But you kissed me because of her," she persisted, because she had to maintain the fight. She could not start thinking about what he did need from her.

"I kissed you because I'd been wanting to ever since we met."

"Even though you thought I was pregnant with Hugh Harrington's baby?"

"I never wanted to believe that. *This* is what I wanted to believe." Again he brushed the bare skin at her shoulder, this time as a deliberate demonstration of the man-woman awareness, the lightning streak of sunfire that burned in her nerve endings. "This chemistry, Isabelle, and the honesty I believed in your eyes."

"Honesty?" She wanted to laugh, to scoff, but her bravado was going up in flames. "How can you believe that anything between us is genuine?"

This time he turned his hand, cupping her shoulder, clouding her resolve with the textured heat of his skin and his voice. "Would you be more inclined to believe if I demonstrated?"

"No," she said quickly. Too quickly. She drew in a calming breath. "There is nothing to prove."

"I disagree. You are sceptical of my intent." He took her hand, twined their fingers, used that leverage to pull her closer. "What if I kissed you again, with no audience and no ulterior motive?"

"Except to prove your point. Madeleine might be—"

"Forget Madeleine."

"—used to having whatever she wants," she continued

strongly over his interjection, "but you are no better. I think you two have a lot in common. You should reconsider."

"You are right on one score. I have grown used to having what I want, and I am honest enough to admit that I want you." He stroked his thumb over the corner of her mouth. "How about you, Isabelle?"

She knew a challenge when it looked her in the eye, and this challenge held her gaze with unflinching boldness. Then he slid his hand from her shoulder to the bare skin of her back. A caress, an encouragement, a gentle pressure that brought her forward to meet his lowering mouth. "One little kiss," he whispered against her lips, "as proof this chemistry is real."

One. Little. Kiss.

Oh, no, this was so much more. It started where the last kiss had ended, a sweet, sensual seduction of her lips and her senses, but as soon as she surrendered—as soon as the hands that had come up to ward him off yielded to the temptation to touch—it plunged into so much more. It was a bold and thorough exploration of lips and tongues and skin, a yielding and a taking and a hunger that ripped through Isabelle the instant her mouth opened beneath his. She felt the tremor deep in her body, heard his throaty sound of satisfaction, tasted the satisfaction in a big dizzying gulp of acknowledgement.

This *was* real, this chemistry, this mutual wanting.

Then his hands took possession, pulling her onto his lap, drawing her tight against the hard heat of his body. It was shockingly raw and primal, his hands on her thighs, thumbs tracing the edge of her invisible knickers as he licked into her mouth. She shifted in his lap, finding a better angle for the kiss and a closer contact with the hard proof of his desire.

Lost in the potency of the moment, she forgot time, place, propriety, the thousand cautions she'd issued herself over the past days. She was greedy for more, for her hands on more than his shirt, more than his throat and his face. She wanted to feel his heat without barriers. She was too close, not close enough. She itched with the craziness of need, and when he swore softly the foreign word, his exasperation, the exhalation of breath hot against her skin, only inflamed her more. She turned in his lap, hands on his shirt buttons, her laugh a husky reflection of her impatience until she realised that he'd gone still and why he'd sworn.

His hands were no longer on her thighs but restraining her hands. The car was stationary, not as part of the slow crawl home through London traffic but because they had arrived at Wentworth Square. And someone was knocking at the car window.

Calmly Cristo shifted her to the seat beside him and straightened her dress, but when he opened the window he took her hand in a reassuring grip. She sucked in a deep breath, the world stopped spinning and the dark figure outside materialised into Crash's craggy features.

"This had better be good," Cristo said darkly.

"Hugh called," the butler replied shortly. "From Farnborough."

Pressed close against his side, Isabelle felt his muscles tense as his irritation with the interruption turned to instant alertness. "I thought he wasn't due back until the weekend."

"Apparently he called Amanda last night, and she mentioned Isabelle."

"Of course she did."

"He's on his way here now. I thought you should know."

Isabelle hadn't thought that anything could wipe that kiss so quickly from her mind. This news had managed the impossible. Uncaring about her kissed-clean lips and mussed hair, she leaned forward into view. "Does Chessie know?"

"She was in the room when the call came in. She's waiting in the library."

Waiting for Hugh's arrival was torture. A diplomatic Crash suggested that she might like to "freshen up," but she shook her head. Nobody cared if her ridiculously expensive dress was slightly crumpled, her feet bare, her hair and makeup ravaged. Chessie hadn't even noticed, a sure indication that despite her outward signs of preparedness and her assurances that she was more than ready for this meeting, her sister was jangling with nerves.

Isabelle forced her to sit and practice her breathing. "It's never too early," she said, taking her sister's hand and demonstrating with a couple of exaggerated Lamaze-inspired breaths. Chessie laughed and almost relaxed until they heard someone outside the door and her grip turned almost punishing with sudden tension.

But it was only Crash bringing them tea, and a few minutes later Cristo returned from the male version of freshening up, which meant he no longer looked as though he'd been run over by a wildly turned-on woman. He'd changed into jeans and a light sweater. His eyes found Isabelle's right away, steady, questioning, and she nodded a silent answer. *We're good.* And she realised with a warm settling of her own nerves that this wasn't a platitude, that with the calming strength of his presence they would get through this.

He took a chair opposite and distracted them both by asking Chessie about her visit to the National Gallery and then updating them on his horse Gisele's improving health. He was so easy to listen to, so easy to watch as he explained the rudiments of polo to Chessie with words and hands and a stray ball he found on the desk. Chessie relaxed enough to ask questions, to laugh at his answers, although every so often her gaze flicked to the window overlooking the street.

When the doorbell rang, she lifted an inch off the sofa. "He's here."

Her words were superfluous—who else would be calling after midnight?—and barely audible despite the sudden silence. Cristo stood, his tension marked in the rigid set of his jaw and the flexing of his hands into fists. She wondered if that was merely an easing of tension or a sign of intent, but she could not feel any alarm on Hugh Harrington's part. He deserved whatever was coming.

In the hallway outside they heard voices, Crash's and another, but when Isabelle reached for Chessie's hand, her sister shook her head. "I'm good," she said. "I can do this."

When the door opened and Crash stepped back to usher in the new arrival, Isabelle's eyes remained on Chessie's face. She saw her sister's slight recoil, the small shake of her head as she looked from Hugh to Crash to Cristo. He was the first to speak, his voice as hard and dark as the ebony timber that dominated the room.

"Hugh," he said. "I'm glad you saw fit to return home and face the music."

"No." Chessie was still shaking her head as she looked from one man to the other. "What's going on? This is not Harry."

Ten

Cristo watched the bewilderment on every face following Francesca's declaration and Hugh's equally adamant avowal that he was, as recently as one hour ago when his passport was last checked, Hugh Harrington. When Francesca argued that point, Hugh reached into an inside pocket and produced the document, which Chessie refused to look at.

"Are you Isabelle Browne?" Hugh asked, and Cristo had to step in and referee the confused melee of answers. Finally he managed to explain, to everyone's satisfaction, the story of the sister swap in Melbourne.

"I am the pregnant one," Francesca reiterated in case anyone was still in doubt. "But you are not my Harry."

"No, I'm not," Hugh said thoughtfully, and then he laughed softly with what sounded like wonderment. "I'll be damned."

"What?" Cristo asked at the same time as Isabelle.

"I am *a* Harry," Hugh replied, and Cristo went still.

"Justin?" he asked sharply.

Hugh nodded. "He flew to Melbourne for the auction."

"He stayed at this client's house?"

"Just for one night."

"Apparently that was enough," Cristo murmured.

"Who are you talking about?" Isabelle stepped forward, her forehead creased in confusion. She placed her hand on Cristo's arm and instantly had his attention. "Are there other Harrys?"

"Justin is Hugh's elder brother. I didn't know they shared the nickname. It didn't cross my mind that it could be Justin."

"I'll say." Hugh still looked bemused. "Would never have picked it."

"Why not?" Francesca asked into the beat of pause that followed this announcement. "Please don't tell me he is married or engaged or a serial—"

"No," Hugh cut in. "Justin isn't married, at least not anymore."

Under a barrage of questions, the story finally came together. Hugh had been Harringtons' man in situ in Australia back in January, doing the groundwork for a major estate sale. Justin arrived to oversee the auction before flying back to New York. According to Hugh, that encapsulated his brother's life since the death of his wife last summer—constant travel, little sleep, working like an automaton. Which is why it had never crossed his mind that Justin could be the "Harry" Francesca sought.

Yes, they'd both been dubbed Harry at school, as had their father and grandfather and all Harrington men since time immemorial, but the nickname hadn't stuck to Justin. Cristo understood why. Unlike his younger brother, Justin Harrington had never been one of the party-hard players around town. He'd always been serious—not a Harry but a Lord Justin Harrington, viscount and future earl, head of a traditional and ultra-conservative family business.

And, according to Hugh, he'd become a complete social hermit since Leesa's tragic boating accident. "To the best of my knowledge, he has not even casually dated," he confided to Cristo. "Must say I'm somewhat flummoxed by this evidence to the contrary. Do you think Chessie is on the up-and-up?"

"Do you think I would have brought her here from Australia and put her up in my home if I didn't?"

"From what Amanda says, I thought that might have more to do with the sister."

Cristo didn't give him the benefit of an answer. It didn't matter what any of them thought; the truth would be determined by Justin. Crash had turned up an auction brochure bearing his picture, and Francesca identified him with a conclusive nod before tapping a finger against the advertised sale date. "Is he in New York for this?"

"Not only for the auction," Hugh replied. "A key executive resigned early this year. Left the Manhattan office in a bit of a jumble."

"Is he expected home soon?"

"For the wedding. But with the Carmichael sale only days before, there's some doubt he'll even make the rehearsal. Your best bet would be to call him, although I wonder…" Harry ruminated for several seconds, his expression turning from thoughtful to diffident. "I wonder if you would mind terribly much if we kept this under our hats, as it were, until after the wedding. Justin is my best man, and I would rather he were at my side than dashing you off to Vegas."

"That is not going to happen," Francesca said with feeling.

"Then I beg you not to break this news to my family before the wedding."

"Will they run me out of town?" she asked. "Or force me to the altar with a shotgun?"

Hugh reassured her that neither would be the case, although they might expect a wedding before the baby. "Rather old-fashioned in that regard," he said, "but you've nothing to fear. Justin will insist on doing the responsible thing. That's why I'm concerned about telling him now, you see. It's not only the wedding—this Carmichael sale is crucial to Harringtons' reputation in America. Your news would prove somewhat of a distraction, I'm afraid."

"Another two weeks won't make any difference to me," Francesca replied, "except we may have overstayed our welcome here."

"Not at all," Cristo assured her evenly. "You should not feel pressured to rush yourself from under my roof or to accept Hugh's request for a delay. I can fly you to New York."

"Thank you, but I don't want to turn this into a chase around the world. I can wait until after the wedding." She rested a hand on her belly. "I have months of patience left."

Isabelle attempted to argue, but Francesca's mind was made up. Pleading tiredness, she excused herself and went upstairs, her stormy-faced sister at her side. A satisfied Harry left soon after, but Cristo was neither satisfied nor ready to retire. He had a feeling Isabelle would return—she would want to pursue this new development, to know where she and Francesca stood—and he did not have long to wait for her knock at the door.

"Can I pour you a cognac?" he asked, ushering her across the room to the massive ebony desk where Crash had left a tray bearing bottle and glasses. She looked pale, agitated, in need of both a drink and reassurance.

"Does it help?"

"It certainly doesn't hurt." When he passed her the glass, their fingers brushed and a frisson of heated memory flickered across her face. Cristo's body stirred in response, but he said nothing; this was not the time. Leaning back against the desk, he watched her take a tentative sip. Accepted her murmured thanks.

"Not only for the drink," she added, swirling the golden liquid for a second before taking a visible grip of her fretfulness. "You were very fair, offering Chessie the opportunity to go to New York."

"Did you manage to change her mind?"

She laughed ruefully and shook her head. "I'm afraid I have never had much success on that score."

"Tonight must have been quite a shock for her. Perhaps she needs the extra time to adjust to this turn of events. To allow this new picture of her baby's father to take shape."

"Can I ask…" She turned her glass a slow, measured circle within her hands and inhaled deeply. "Is he everything Hugh suggested?"

"Justin is a decent man, highly thought of, honourable. Francesca and her baby are in good hands."

She took her time digesting that, but gradually the storm in her eyes settled as if she'd accepted his judgement. A small thing, Cristo told himself, to produce such inordinate pleasure. "You must be happy with how this has turned out," she said. "Given the alternative."

Oddly, he hadn't given any consideration to what had been averted. Not until now. The ramifications for Amanda and Hugh were huge, and that realisation ramped his pleasure to a new level and brought a smile to his lips. "This drink should be a celebration." He leaned closer, touched his glass to hers. "To satisfactory solutions."

"And happy endings," she added, "for everyone."

Cristo toasted that, but she must have noticed the unspoken cynicism in his salute because her gaze drifted away and the smile tugging at the corners of her mouth faltered. She sipped at her drink, swallowed, swirled, before her gaze lifted again to his. "What now?" she asked. "How are we to keep this secret until after the wedding? Amanda is so…"

"Nosy?"

"She is curious because she cares about you and she thinks we are a couple. She invited me to lunch next week. She pressed me to commit to a day, and she asked if I was coming to her wedding. I can't keep lying to her, and if she meets Chessie and notices she is pregnant… I can't keep up this pretence for two weeks, Cristo. I think it would be best if we went to stay somewhere else."

"I agree," he said mildly, and she blinked in surprise. He could think of nothing better than taking her somewhere else, a place with no Amanda, no Francesca, no Harrys of any variety. "I was wanting to spend this weekend at Chisholm Park. You will come with me," he decided. Not the perfect solution, but one Cristo could warm to…especially if he could ensure they were left alone.

"But won't that defeat the purpose?"

"The purpose being?"

"To avoid Amanda's attempts to embrace me into your family. I was thinking Chessie and I should go somewhere remote—a hotel or a B and B."

"Somewhere I'm not?" he challenged. "Is that more to the point, Isabelle?"

"No," she retorted quickly. "I was only questioning whether Amanda and your mother and the bridal party would be descending on your family home for the wedding."

"Thankfully, no. Our village church wouldn't accommodate the masses, so the wedding is in Sussex, near the Harrington estate. I can assure you that the wedding party will be heading south from London, in the opposite direction to us."

She'd been playing with her drink again, turning the glass within her hands, but they stilled on the last word. Her gaze lifted to his. "Does *us* include Chessie?"

"She is welcome," he replied. "Although earlier she mentioned how much she is enjoying London and the galleries."

"Her idea of heaven."

"Then perhaps she would prefer to stay here."

She took less than a second to catch on, for her shoulders to straighten. "You would prefer her to stay here. Be honest— that is what you are really saying, isn't it?"

"I would prefer you to myself, Isabelle, with no interruptions."

His voice slowed and deepened, his message clearly reflected in her eyes. Suddenly they were back in the car, his hands on her thighs, hers fumbling with his buttons, their breathing hot and impatient. But when he signalled his intent to act, putting down his glass with a decisive thunk and shifting his body weight to his feet, she backed away. Just a few steps before she changed course, circling around to put the huge desk between them.

From that position of safety, she levelled him a steady gaze. "What are you proposing?"

"A weekend in the country, no pretence or coercion, just you and me and a dozen polo ponies. As to what else..." Without losing eye contact, he reached down and snagged the polo ball from the desk. He rolled it slowly across the impressive breadth of timber and into her hands. "That ball is yours to play, Isabelle. I'm in your hands."

"I don't need you as a babysitter, and you know it. You're using me as an excuse," Chessie accused after hearing of last night's invitation. Isabelle had badgered her sister into accompanying her on a morning walk—not Chessie's favourite activity—to talk about her reaction to "Harry's" surprise identity. But within a block Chessie had hijacked the conversation and turned the walk into a stroll. Feigning fatigue, she sunk to a bench in the centre of the square and narrowed her perceptive eyes on Isabelle's still-standing figure. "You're afraid of what might happen. A whole weekend alone with the delicious Cristo. You are such a chicken."

"You're a fine one to talk about cowardice," Isabelle countered hotly. She couldn't sit; she itched with the need to keep walking, to clear her woolly head after a sleepless night. To feel like her normal, sensible self again. "You could have gone to New York. You've already flown halfway around the world to find this man."

"And what I found out last night is enough for now. Give me a week to digest all that…."

"A week? Your decisions usually take less than a second."

"Usually I'm not considering anything more important than blue dress or skinny jeans." Chessie's eyes held hers, her expression serious for at least a second before she gave a rueful shrug. "Course, in a few days I'll probably wish I had taken up Cristo's generous offer, but for now I'm happy with my choice. You, on the other hand, are not."

Trust her little sister to see right through her restless irritability. Last night Cristo hadn't accepted what he called her knee-jerk answer. Initially that had revolved around her employment contract—how could she go away for a weekend when her job was to keep Chessie and Amanda apart?

He'd responded by giving her the weekend off and suggesting she sleep on it—ha!—and he would ask again when he returned from wherever he'd flown today. He'd told her where, but the name was unfamiliar and possibly unspellable. Yet another sign, she'd reasoned during the hours she'd lain awake and then paced her spacious bedroom, of the disparity in their lifestyles. Yet another reason to resist this mad attraction.

"I'm not happy because of all this." She gestured widely around her, at the rows of stately town houses, the chauffeur opening the door of a Rolls Royce at number twelve, the woman emerging decked head to foot in high couture. She waved her hand at her own chain-store jeans. "Belgravia is not me, Chess."

"Then perhaps you need a break in the country."

"You think Chisholm Park will be anything less?"

"How do you know? Aren't you curious, just a little bit?"

"No," Isabelle snapped. But when Chessie caught her hand and tugged, she subsided to the seat at her side. She sighed heavily. "Not a bit curious. A lot."

Ever since he'd told her that Chisholm Park was his home, and she'd sensed his impatience to be there. That hunger to know more had been fed last night, when he'd diverted Chessie with news of Gisele and polo and she'd eaten up every scrap of information. She remembered the man in Melbourne, so pumped and fizzing with earthy vitality after a morning riding with Judd Armitage.

This was the man she hungered to know, the real man, the one who'd looked into her eyes last night and spoken with stripped-bare sincerity.

No pretence or coercion, just you and me and a dozen polo ponies.

"I am afraid," she admitted now, "of how much I want to go. You know me, Chess. I don't do weekend romps."

"I know, but what if it's more than that?" Chessie argued. "He's invited you to his home."

Isabelle scoffed dismissively. She had to, to counteract the mad skitter of her heart. "It's only a weekend."

"If that's all it is, then why not go and satisfy your curiosity? What have you got to lose?"

Eleven

Cristo didn't return from places unpronounceable to seek her answer; he sent a car. According to the message delivered midafternoon in a clipped, haven't-a-second-to-waste tone by his executive assistant, he'd been delayed unavoidably. A car would collect her at 8:00 p.m. sharp.

"Like a package to be delivered," Isabelle grumbled after the call's abrupt disconnection. "I wonder if his housekeeper will have to sign for me?"

"Probably won't need to," Chessie replied. "Isn't his country pile quite close to the airport he uses? He might well be there when you're tossed out on the doorstep. Just waiting to unwrap you."

He wasn't.

After spending the interminable stop-start drive on tenterhooks, trying her best not to imagine those clever hands undressing her, Isabelle was left deflated. Not because she was looking forward to that doorstep unwrapping. She was too annoyed by his presumptuous sending of a car. She should have sent it packing; she shouldn't have been swayed by Chessie's prodding or by the whispery hopes of *what if...*.

What if he really did feel the same attraction, the same explosion of sunfire in every touch? What if this was more than chemistry, more than a passing intrigue?

Unfortunately, a part of her had succumbed to that notion. Just a small part, mind, because she was altogether too pragmatic to imagine that plain, ordinary, been-nowhere, done-nothing Isabelle Browne could be anything but a momentary novelty to a man like Cristo Verón. Another part of her—a hot, dangerous, newly awakened part—ached to be that passing novelty. She'd always thought ahead, made the sensible choices, gone with the unselfish options. If she was ever going to throw caution to the wind and do something just to please herself and hang the consequences, this was her chance.

It was a heady, exciting notion. She could almost hear her sister cheering her on...and that was enough to create huge trepidation. Chessie had a habit of throwing caution to the wind, and now she was dealing with the consequences.

Despite her emotions careening in every direction, somewhere along the A1 Isabelle managed to doze off. She missed the anticipated rush of seeing Chisholm Park for the first time, which only added to the disappointment of being met by the housekeeper. Meredith, a tall, stylish redhead who didn't wear a uniform, told her that Cristo would not be home for hours yet. There followed a quick tour of the house, peppered by directions of "this room is" and "over there you'll find" that Isabelle was too unfocussed to take aboard.

After Isabelle declined the offer of supper, tea or anything from the kitchen, Meredith prepared to leave. "Cristo said you should make yourself at home. Do you remember where everything is? The kitchen and the library and his sitting room with the big-screen tele?"

Isabelle said yes, she remembered, since she had no intention of exploring the endless corridors or of sitting up to welcome him home. Unsure whether she would stay, she didn't unpack. She took her time preparing for bed; she imagined she would still be tossing and turning long after eleven. But after a cursory round of tosses and turns, she surrendered to the thick embrace of her down duvet and slept dreamlessly until after six. For the first time in weeks she felt deeply rested and ready to face the day. Outside birds chattered with early morning industry, but the house slept on. She hurried down two flights of stairs and out the front door without drawing breath. She craved her morning walk, her thinking time, before she faced any conversation or decisions.

It was a splendid morning for walking. In the splintered sunlight of the tree-lined driveway, the air was shivery cool despite her sweater and jeans and she set off at a brisk pace, her mind only on the task of exercise. But soon it grew impossible to ignore the birdcalls, and the drumming vibration of an unseen woodpecker slowed her pace as she skimmed the treetops in a vain attempt to locate the creature. As her view widened, she was captured by a cluster of horses, sleek and glossy beneath the clear sky, and as she continued to turn in a slow circle the house came into view and her eyes boggled.

If she'd thought the Belgravia town house was something, then this was something else.

Three storeys of red-brick stateliness stood like a rosy castle amid endless acres of verdant parkland.

"Chisholm Park indeed," she murmured as she scanned the sweeps of grass broken by uncontrived plantings of leafy herbage and trees. Oaks and beeches and ashes—and, over to the west, beyond a dense wooded thicket, she caught the gleam of sunlight on water.

Intrigued, she turned off the driveway and cut across an open field, her stride lengthening as she followed the downhill slope until she found a better vantage point for what turned out to be a small lake. It was picture perfect, a movie set, beyond anything she'd imagined.

Seeking a closer view, she continued on, following a pathway until the ground levelled out. She paused when she heard the distant sound of galloping hooves. Curious, she changed direction through a wooded grove and exited onto a closely mown field where a trio of horses and riders raced in hot pursuit of a polo ball. She recognised it from the one Cristo had rolled across the desk. She recognised Cristo in the same heartbeat, despite the face-shadowing helmet. In white breeches and long tan boots, he manoeuvred his shiny black steed to overtake the others with languid ease.

Isabelle was riveted.

Yes, she'd seen him at polo practice before—she'd commented on his prowess at the Mornington restaurant—but that day she had watched from a distance. She'd not been close enough to feel the ground reverberate beneath thundering hooves, to smell the earthy mix of horse and turf, to hear the urgent calls that signalled the next play. Today she'd wandered right onto the edge of the action, and she watched transfixed as the threesome powered by. Cristo led the charge at breakneck speed, and when he leaned precariously low over the horse's side, her breath caught in alarm.

But with effortless skill he swung the stick in a smooth arc and smacked the ball beneath his horse's neck and out of the others' reach.

They wheeled to follow, and Isabelle's heart resumed beating with renewed exhilaration. Grinning widely, she lifted her hands to applaud and then realised that the ball was rocketing across the grass toward her. She didn't want to interrupt their practice; she would have scooted back into the shelter of the trees, but then Cristo spotted her.

His head came up, a new alertness in his posture, and Isabelle knew his gaze had locked on her. She felt the ripple of awareness down her spine, the jump of her pulse, the curl of honeyed heat in her stomach, and she couldn't move. With an infinitesimal lift of his hands, he slowed his horse, and she heard him call the others to stop play.

The ball's pace slowed on the thicker outer grass, and Isabelle's heart thumped hard as she threw caution to the wind and took a decisive step to meet it. Intent on her rash purpose—would she roll it back or hand it to him?—she didn't notice the approaching horse until it cut through her path. The mallet's powerful swing was so near she felt the shift of air in its wake.

As she jumped out of harm's way, the rider lifted her head, and she recognised the venomous smirk of crimson lips. Madeleine. She recoiled reflexively, the punch of shock driving all the breath and heat and exhilaration from her body. Vaguely she registered the cold bark of anger in Cristo's voice as he called Madeleine to task, and then he was cantering toward her and vaulting from the saddle and striding to her side.

She was pretty sure he would have wrapped her in his arms if she'd not taken an evasive step and held up both hands to ward him off. She didn't want cosseting, and she didn't need his soothing sounds of concern. "I'm fine," she assured him, her voice brittle with sudden anger. "Obviously she needs the practice. Her shot was way off."

He cursed, or at least that's what she gathered. The word was foreign—she was going on tone and the way he ripped off his helmet and glove and tossed them the way of his mallet. Helmet hair, she noted snippily, but then he raked a hair through the flattened crown and turned his fierce gaze on her and for a moment her synapses tied themselves in knots. Which, when she started to think again, only made her madder.

"I'm going to resume my walk now. Is it safe to continue this way—" she indicated the path along the side of the field "—or should I go back the way I came?"

"I'll walk with you," he said.

"Protection? Is that necessary?"

She started to move away, but he stopped her with a hand on her shoulder, turning her back toward him. She felt like slapping the hand away, but beyond his broad shoulders she could see the two horses, two riders, waiting and watching. She was not about to give Madeleine and friend the benefit of front-row seats to any display of disillusioned fury.

"You had a right to be angry, even before Madeleine's stunt," he said. "I meant what I said about this weekend. I didn't invite her here."

"You don't owe me any explanation," she said tightly.

"Yes, I do." Cupping both shoulders, he held her steady. Forced her to meet his gaze. "Madeleine is playing in a charity tournament tomorrow. This morning she discovered that one of her ponies is lame. She needs a replacement."

"And she thought of you."

"She thought of me, the team sponsor, who she knows is not playing tomorrow and will therefore have spare ponies."

Oh. She swallowed. "Why aren't you playing?" she couldn't resist asking.

"I have other plans."

Those other plans pulsed between them for a long moment, and Isabelle felt a change in his grip, saw a new tension in the set of his jaw. He was waiting for her to object, to tell him that her plans had suddenly changed, and three seconds ago he would have been right on the money. But now… "You were going to play?" she asked, needing to know for sure. "Until these other plans came along?"

"Yes."

"You didn't have to do that on my account. I might have enjoyed a day at the polo."

"With Madeleine playing?" he asked dryly. "Not a good idea."

"She wasn't meaning to run me down." The ache of conflict eased from her chest and suddenly she felt magnanimous, even toward Madeleine. "She knew there was room to spare."

Again his grip tightened and so did the corners of his mouth. "Whatever she meant, it was a foolhardy stunt. I shouldn't have let her onto the field this morning. She was already in a snit."

"Because you're not playing tomorrow?" she guessed.

"Because of my replacement," he corrected.

"Is there someone else she dislikes as much as me, or is it because the stand-in is not as good a player?"

He laughed, the sound unexpected and acutely sexy. "My replacement is the great Alejandro Verón. He is a ten-goal player."

"This is better than you?"

"That's as good as it gets," he said. "My brother is a professional. I don't play nearly enough to approach his standard."

He spoke as a matter of fact, not arrogant, just supremely confident that with sufficient games he too would be one of the best. Isabelle wondered if there was anything he didn't do supremely well. A shiver danced through her, and when his gaze narrowed intently and the tenor of his grip changed, she knew he'd sensed it, seen it... For whatever reason, he knew. Perhaps it glowed like an aura of lust around her.

It was too much, too soon, and she flicked her gaze toward his horse. Still standing, obediently still, where he'd been abandoned, except... "Is your horse supposed to be eating your glove?" she asked slowly.

Amusement glimmered in his eyes as they flicked over the horse and then returned to her face. "Perhaps he is hungry. Have *you* eaten, Isabelle?"

Her stomach had bottomed out. Hunger, yes, although not only for food. "Not yet."

"Let's return to the stables, and then I will treat you to the best breakfast in the home counties."

The village pub was only a couple of kilometres across country. They could have walked, and another day they would, but by the time they'd finished up at the stables and he'd showered and changed, Cristo was starving. He grabbed Isabelle's hand and tugged her toward the garage. When she caught sight of the array of vehicles, he had to tug even harder.

"Are these all yours?" she asked. It was the same question and the same awed expression as when she'd walked into the stables and clocked all the heads poking out into the central alley.

"Not this time." He towed her toward his Aston and popped the doors. "This one's mine. The rest were Alistair's. They're Amanda's now. She hasn't the heart to sell them."

When he gunned the car down the drive, he spied Isabelle stroking the leather seat and that brought out a satisfied grin. "It does that, doesn't it?"

Their eyes met and shared the moment, the purr of the powerful engine, the warmth of a perfect May morning, the silent promise of the weekend ahead. He reached for her hand, felt the rocket of response from that simple touch. "I'm glad you came," he said.

"And if I hadn't?"

"I would have driven to London. I would have changed your mind."

Breakfast was in the restaurant attached to a quaint village pub that was full of old English charm and customers. Unsurprising, really, given the breakfast was as good as Cristo had promised. They ate and they talked, picking up the conversation started on the short drive.

Isabelle discovered more about Chisholm Park, including how Alistair had bought the place as a failed means of keeping Vivi happy. He'd renovated extensively, adding stables for horse-mad Cristo and a poolhouse for Amanda and the lake for his wife. "And for himself?" Isabelle asked.

"He chose this location convenient to the headquarters of Chisholm Air. When marriage failed him, the business he loved did not."

She learned more about the business, casual information interspersed with telling observations that suggested Cristo had inherited his stepfather's love of Chisholm Air along with his chairmanship and stock holdings. Isabelle's mood was a peculiar mix of comfort from the easy conversation and gathering despair because every anecdote reinforced the disparity in their positions and their beliefs.

His cynicism toward love and marriage and his attitude to business do not matter, she reminded herself. *This is makebelieve. Just enjoy the moment.*

A neighbour stopped by their table and asked about the prospects of the Chisholm Hawks in tomorrow's tournament.

Briefly they analysed the competition, expert opinion maintaining that if Cristo's brother was in form, the Hawks would win with several goals to spare. "See you tomorrow, then," Will said, "and you, Isabelle."

"I hope so." She returned his hearty smile, then watched him leave.

"I trust you were only being polite."

"Yes…and no." Isabelle worried at her bottom lip. "Look, I know you're not playing and that was on my behalf, but from what Will said, this Sovereign's Plate tournament is a big deal, and your brother's appearance even more so."

"I can see A.J. anytime," he said with an offhand shrug, but there was nothing casual in the banked heat of his gaze when it lifted from her mouth to her eyes. "Unless there is a reason you want to go to tomorrow's game?"

"Other than meeting your brother?"

"You don't want to meet him."

"Why ever not?" Isabelle asked, her curiosity piqued. "Are you alike?"

"I'm told there is a resemblance, but only in appearance. I am the good brother," he said, an edge of humour sparking his dark eyes.

"And Alejandro is bad?"

"The worst."

"Is this why I don't want to meet him?"

"This is why I do not want you to meet him," he said, and the possessiveness of that statement caused a delicious tightening in her stomach. A heaviness in her breasts. And the certainty that this brother—the good one—could make her feel very, very bad. "Nor do I intend sharing you with every inquisitive neighbour who stops by."

"Isn't that what you wanted me for at the gala?"

"Unless you want me to remind you exactly what I want—" again those eyes glittered, again her body tightened "—with half of Herting Green leaning sideways in their chairs to eavesdrop, I suggest we get out of here."

"Will you tell me, then?"

"Better than that, Isabelle. I will show you."

Twelve

He showed her with a steamy kiss the instant they were cocooned in the privacy of his car. It was hot and open-mouthed, a kiss packed with carnal intent and controlled aggression, the kiss they'd started in the backseat of the limo turned up another ten notches.

It was exactly what Isabelle needed to wipe her mind free of the nagging what-the-hell-are-you-doing-here? doubts that had resurfaced while he settled the bill.

Closing her eyes to the late-morning brightness, she surrendered instantly, completely, absorbing the scent of leather and man, the enticing pressure of his thumbs at the corners of her mouth, the strong taste of coffee on his tongue. She'd given up the brew, fearing her reliance, and now she knew the taste would be forever etched in this long, hot tangle of mouths and the shudder of longing deep in her core.

When he finally broke away, the passion of their embrace

throbbed in the overheated air and in the dark smoulder of his eyes. "Home?" he asked.

"Yes."

Two words, their first since he'd ushered her from the restaurant, and perfectly enough. He strapped their seat belts and started the engine, and the Aston's bark of response echoed through her blood. Pulling out of the car park, they had to wait for an elderly lady to pass. Cristo's fingers drummed an impatient beat on the steering wheel. Isabelle wondered if her need was as nakedly apparent.

Across the street, a family exited the village store, two children intent on ice creams, their mother on talking a toddler down from a tantrum. A normal day, with people going about their Saturday morning activities, while she was being whisked back to a country estate in a midnight-blue Aston Martin by a polo-playing millionaire.

That should have freaked her out, but she felt unusually confident. She also knew that her emotions could quickly cartwheel out of control, especially if she allowed herself to think. "Do you have music?" she asked.

He flicked…something…and the seductive rhythms of Ravel filled the silence.

She smiled at the choice, and when he lifted an enquiring brow, she told him how she'd imagined his entrance music as Ravel the day he arrived in Melbourne. "Not 'La Valse,'" she added, recognising the obsessive darkness in this piece. "Something smoother."

"I saw you dancing that day," he said. Her eyes widened in surprise. "Past one of the windows. You were not what I expected."

"What were you expecting?"

"Superficial beauty…the kind that used to attract Hugh."

"I didn't strike you as Hugh's type?"

"No." Briefly his glance left the road, caught on hers. "You struck me as mine."

Then he reached for her hand, brought it to his thigh, and the hard muscle shifting with every gear change honed her desire to a sharp edge. She wanted both hands on him without the denim barrier—without any barrier—and she wanted his hands on her and his undiverted gaze when she asked him to tell her again.

You struck me as mine.

She'd been achingly aware of him, of his eyes following her as she'd shown him around the house, but she'd never allowed herself to believe it was personal. That he might be drawn to her despite her ugly grey uniform. But when he turned off the engine in the garage and unbuckled his belt and then hers, perhaps he saw the hint of wonder in her eyes because he paused and his expression narrowed.

"You are not having second thoughts," he said. No question, a statement of fact.

"No." Isabelle swallowed, unaccountably nervous despite the certainty of her response. "Although now might be a very good time to remind me of what you want."

"In words?"

"That would depend on the words."

"Indeed," he said slowly, drawing the word out and studying her with enough erotic speculation to burn the clothes from her body. Words did not matter when he looked at her that way, or when he turned an ordinary word into a thing of honeyed beauty with his clever tongue.

All the way from garage to bedroom he put that tongue to wicked purpose, telling her in rich, raw detail exactly what he wanted to do with her, to her, in her. Halfway up the stairs, he paused to study her feverish face. "Hot?" he asked.

She managed a strangled *hmm* of assent, so he peeled away her sweater and camisole in one smooth motion. The glancing heat of his hands against her skin almost brought her to her knees. The flare of his nostrils as he studied the swollen rise of her breasts did cause her thighs to tremble. She might have melted right there, a pool of undone woman on the ornate staircase, if he'd not scooped her up in his arms.

It was so unexpected that she released a breath of surprised laughter. "You didn't mention your need to carry me."

"Humour me."

"Happy to."

He'd reached the landing and paused, his expression all male satisfaction as he looked into her face. "On all counts?"

The detail of his very specific requests burned hot in her skin, but her female parts danced with unembarrassed excitement. She smiled, a softly wanton curve of her lips that caused Cristo's nostrils to flare and his eyes to glitter with piercing heat. "Are we starting with the staircase?" she asked.

"We are starting in my bed."

"And finishing where?"

"Paradise."

She laughed, an earthy ripple of sound that stroked every massively aroused cell in Cristo's body. He felt like he'd been hard for hours, days, weeks. He felt like he could remain so, riding this crest of desire until he could no longer stand, until there were no ways left to have her. One weekend was too finite, too short, and the thought tore at his patience.

He shouldered open the door to his suite, kicked it shut behind them, and the solid thud shut down the clamour for instant gratification. He did not want quick, not this first time. He wanted it exactly as he'd spelled out on the stairs.

Slow. Deep. Thorough.

He turned to lower her against the door, holding her upright between the hard throb of his body and the thick slab of timber. He kissed her with the laughter fresh on her lips, lost himself in the sweet passion of her mouth and then in the torturous ache of her hands on his skin. They'd burrowed beneath his shirt to skim his back, his shoulders, the curve of his biceps, but it was not enough.

"Pull it off," he breathed between kisses, and when she'd dispensed with his shirt the spill of her breasts from low-cut lace burned against his chest. He held her higher, enough that he could lick at the swell of flesh and tug the engorged nipple between his teeth. She cried out, a tortured pant of wanting, and he obliged, dedicating himself to each breast in turn until she writhed beneath him.

He needed skin against skin.

Dios, he ached to be inside her.

She hooked arms and legs around him as he carried her to the bed, as he pulled back and discarded the covers and took her down onto the cool sheets. He reared back, enough to strip her of bra and jeans and underpants, enough to dispense of his, and then they came together in a crackle of lust. The perfection of her softly rounded body, the mix of vanilla sweetness and earthy spices, the throaty gasp of his name on her lips when his fingers delved between her legs—everything about her drove him crazy with greed. He could not kiss her in enough places, caress her long enough, when all he wanted was everything at once.

When she took him in her hands, her touch was a contradictory mix of boldness and explorative innocence that snapped his restraint. He pressed a long, hot kiss to her mouth, to each breast, to the feminine curve of her belly, and then he rolled away to don protection. She arched up to meet his return, and he linked their hands and stretched them high above their heads as he lowered himself between her thighs and sunk into her welcoming heat.

"Look at me," he said thickly, compelling Isabelle's gaze back to his as he slid deeper and started to move in a slow, rolling pace that sealed their connection and rocked against every sweet spot. He maintained that deep eye contact when he took her mouth, when he kissed her with the same sensual rhythm, and when she arched her back with the first shuddering grasp of her climax, he could no longer control his response.

The tension gathered in every muscle, coiled around the base of his spine, and her fingers clung tightly to his as his synapses snapped with the powerful surge of his release.

Isabelle hated the aftermath of sex. She didn't know how to act, what to say, whether to speak at all. To her inexperienced mind, there seemed dangers at every turn, when the mind turned mushy with lust suddenly clicked back to clarity and thought, *Uh-oh. Was I too wanton, too passive, too needy? Should I ask after the nail marks in his hand, offer to apply Band-Aids if I broke the skin? Is it better to take my cue from him, or to be proactive and ask what happens next?*

And that was without the practical aspects of retrieving clothes strewn from here to midday.

God, she'd let him strip her on the stairs.

The thought of Meredith finding her things on the staircase caused her to jackknife upright. Cristo hadn't said anything since returning from the bathroom; she'd wondered if he might be asleep, but she felt the weight of his hand on her back, the gliding touch of his fingertips against her shoulder blade. "What is it?" he asked. His voice sounded heavy with a yawn, and that very human sign gave her the courage to turn and meet his gaze.

"I just remembered my clothes are on the stairs," she admitted.

The mild enquiry in his eyes turned warmly teasing. "And your tidy housekeeper's mind is offended?"

"I was thinking more of your housekeeper, actually. I don't want her picking up after me or thinking…"

"That you're spending the day in bed with me? I'm sure Meredith wouldn't give that a second thought."

Because she's used to it? Isabelle wanted to ask, but didn't. Afraid the miserable jab of jealousy might show in her face, she looked away. "I would rather she didn't find them," she said stiffly, "that's all."

The weight of his hand shifted, its pressure encouraging her to relax back into the pillows. She resisted, waiting for his response. "Unless you leave them there until Monday," he said, "none of my staff will find them."

"Don't they work on the weekends?"

"Not this one. I told you, Isabelle," he continued when her gaze shifted back to his, "I planned for these days to be just us."

He hadn't wanted any staff on duty. Because of all the places he wanted to strip her? To have her? Heat bloomed beneath her skin at the memory of his incendiary words, of each and every steamy promise. "Were you that confident?"

"No," he replied, but his expression, his posture, his satisfied smile were all supremely confident. "I was more…hopeful."

"Did your hopefulness extend to us ending up here in your bed after you took me to breakfast?"

"This has pretty much ruined my plans for today."

Teasing, Isabelle knew, so she took no umbrage. "What had you planned?"

"A long drive."

"To show me the sites of Hertfordshire?"

"To have you to myself, to let the Aston work its magic.

For sightseeing, nothing beats a helicopter," he added, "especially when you take along a picnic and put down wherever takes your fancy."

"That was quite a day you had planned," Isabelle said, impressed despite herself.

"I thought I would have my work cut out," he admitted, and although his tone maintained the lightness of the preceding banter, there was something in his gaze that coiled tight in Isabelle's stomach. Then he grinned, a ridiculously sexy and satisfied smile that belied any question of doubt. "For you, Isabelle, I had planned a serious day of wooing."

Wooing. It was such a delightfully old-fashioned word and such a romantic notion that Isabelle couldn't help being charmed. She would not allow the tender loop of warmth to take hold, however, because it was only a word…a word wrapped up in that cockiest of grins. His plan had been to woo her into his bed, not to romance her, and for that he'd needed no fancy props. He'd only needed the beguiling directness of his tongue.

"You don't have to impress me with grand gestures," she said, "or with your expensive toys."

"Not even the helicopter?"

"Not even."

"I see." The tilt of his smile shifted from cocky to unholy as his hand drifted from her shoulders to the small of her back. "In that case, I shall have to impress you in other ways."

"Will this involve us leaving this bed?"

His fingertips traced the curve of her buttocks. A languid, tantalising signal of intent. "Not for a very long time."

"Stay," Chessie implored on Monday morning. "There is no reason not to."

Only guilt, Isabelle thought, because when Cristo suggested that she stay on at Chisholm Park until the wedding, her acceptance had come easily and without any consideration for her sister's plight. Perhaps because he'd asked while looking deep into her eyes and filling her just as deeply with the heavy heat of his desire.

"Why don't you come out here?" Isabelle said into the phone. "There is no reason not to."

"There is, actually," Chessie replied after a beat of pause. "Colin has tickets to the Chelsea Flower Show."

"Colin?"

"Crash. His real name is Colin Ashcroft, but I am so over nicknames. Did you know he was at school with Cristo? And he paints. Seriously good stuff."

Isabelle frowned, uncomfortable with Chessie's familiarity with the intriguing butler. "You're not getting too friendly, are you?"

"Romantically? Good grief, no. Colin is looking after me, which I'm sure is the job he's been assigned with you and Cristo out of town. Plus, he knows people." Chessie managed to imbue those last few words with enough profundity that Isabelle knew she meant Justin Harrington. "I would rather be picking his brain than mouldering away in the country."

After being assured there was little mouldering in Herting Green, Chessie consented to come out early the following week, after she'd pored over all the exhibits and Kew Gardens and several other must-sees for an apprentice landscape designer.

Isabelle tried not to be too selfishly pleased to have Cristo and Chisholm Park to herself for a whole week. She loved the place and the effortlessness with which she fitted in. Even when he was working, sometimes at the Luton offices, sometimes in lengthy phone conferences from home, she didn't rattle around or feel lost. She pitched in and helped Meredith and the stable staff. Chloe was even teaching her to ride on the quietest of ponies. Those regular doses of reality helped balance out the fairy-tale aspects of being Cristo Verón's lover.

She vowed to maintain that make-believe, to keep things light, to remember that he'd not promised anything beyond the wedding, but her vows were tested from day one. That was the polo tournament, when he capitulated to her wishes and took her to see the final games. It should have been easy to keep her perspective, seeing him greeting friends in the posh and privileged crowd, but he moved just as easily amongst the grooms and spent most of the afternoon at Isabelle's side.

She wasn't sure if she liked the frantic pace and violent clashes; she found it easier to watch Cristo, to revel in his exhilaration and the pride he took in Chloe's game. Driving to the grounds she'd learned that his young groom was replacing Madeleine on the team. "I will not allow her to get away with yesterday's stunt," he said shortly. "She put you and the pony in needless danger."

Chloe, it turned out, was well up to the task.

"She's good," Isabelle decided, watching her slight figure ride another player off the ball with fearless gusto. Cristo nodded, an answer to her question and a signal of approval when his brother pounced on the loose ball and fired an effortless goal to put the Hawks into the lead. Whatever else he said was lost in the roar of applause and in Isabelle's response when he swung her up in a close embrace and kissed her soundly. Not a peck but a full-blooded this-is-my-woman kiss for all to see.

"Is that how you celebrate every goal?" she asked.

Cristo's grin grew warm as he slid her down his body until her feet touched ground. "You should see how I celebrate a win."

Isabelle did get to see that night, when he swept her home

and made good with another of his promises. Champagne sipped from her skin, he told her, tasted sweeter than any victory. And Isabelle kept her perspective by noting that the champagne was an obscenely expensive vintage. The stuff of fairy tales, it bore no relation to her real life.

Another day he took her sightseeing in a helicopter bearing the Chisholm Air logo. *His* logo, to all intents and purposes, because he casually admitted that he owned a majority share in the company. She'd figured as much, but this confirmation of his wealth put him in a different stratosphere. One where she could not exist without an oxygen mask or a housekeeper's uniform.

Then he brought her down to reality by taking her to dinner at the village pub, this time on foot so he could introduce her to Gisele, the mare who'd almost died while he was in Melbourne and who was now recuperating nicely. Watching him stroke her neck, listening to the deep affection in his voice as he told her about the pony's courage and bravery, turned Isabelle's heart upside down and inside out.

Another evening he brought home an extravagant picnic basket and drove her in the Aston to a secluded spot by the lake. "I had tickets to Glyndebourne tonight," he admitted later, stretching out beside her on the picnic rug. His hand dipped lazily beneath her skirt. "I hope you don't mind, but they frown on making out on the lawns there."

"Stuffy of them," she replied. "I'm glad we didn't go."

"Because you fancy making out on the grass or because you don't like the opera?"

"I've never been."

His hand drifted higher. "So you're an opera virgin?"

"I guess I am," she managed, although his questing fingertips made her feel very unvirginal.

"How do you know you don't like something you've never tried?"

Isabelle's eyes drifted shut. She didn't want to talk, especially about opera. She wanted those clever fingers to really apply themselves to something she did like. But they'd stilled, and when she peered beneath her lowered lids she found him waiting patiently for her answer. "I don't care much for operatic melodrama," she said. "Had enough of it in my childhood."

"Your parents?" he guessed, giving up the seductive intent and turning her until her face rested on his sun-warmed chest. "Tell me about them."

"It's a long story."

"As is many an opera."

She huffed out a laugh. "Then I guess I will start with the opera, which is where my parents met. Working," she added. "My mother was a moderately successful soprano, my father a set director."

"Your love of music is no accident, then?"

"There was always music," Isabelle said with a shrug. "At home, and the lessons they signed us up for. Piano, drama, voice, art. Luckily neither Chessie nor I had the talent or the desire to pursue them."

"Luckily?"

Usually she hated talking about her upbringing, but in the sun-tinged evening with his hand idly stroking her hair she felt relaxed and encouraged. He wanted to know—he wanted to know *her.* "I would not want the life of my parents," she replied with heartfelt fervour. "They travelled constantly, often not together because they were working on different productions. They didn't even have a home."

"Did you travel with your mother?" he asked. The play of

his hand in her hair was no longer lazy; its weight rested a moment, strong and comforting.

"When I was a baby, yes, but then I needed to start school and my mother was pregnant with Chessie. We moved in with my grandparents in Melbourne—Poppy was alive then, too—and that was a disaster." A rueful smile ghosted across her lips. "So many fights, about everything. My father left and my mother started taking jobs, as well. In the end we just spent more and more time with our grandparents."

"What happened to your parents?"

"They visited between seasons, they sent cards and presents for our birthdays, but then my father died. I don't know what happened, but after the funeral there was a big row—Mother brought this horrid new man with her—and we didn't see her again. It was okay," she hastened to add. "In fact, after all the clashes, there was finally some peace in the house, and Gran…she was wonderful."

"I know."

Intrigued, Isabelle rolled onto her side and pushed up onto her elbow. "How do you know?"

"She taught you everything you know, and look how you turned out."

Isabelle smiled into his eyes, unable to hide the pleasure she took from that compliment. It was the perfect ending to the conversation, the perfect endorsement of the grandmother she'd adored, and when he reached for her, his hand strong and warm on her neck, and drew her down into his kiss, she felt an overwhelming swell of emotion inside.

She loved him, not only for this perfect evening or the connection they'd forged this past week, but because of everything she knew of him. His responsibility to his family, his protectiveness of Amanda, his regard for his staff and his animals, his loyalty to the Delahuntys and his stepfather's memory. Even his exasperated dealings with Vivi reflected his deep affection. Every day there was something else, some new facet, and yet she had barely scraped the surface of Cristo Verón.

There was still so much to learn, and for an instant she felt a mild rush of panic because she had so little time and soon this idyll would be over. But then his hands slid up her thighs to cradle her buttocks, and the kiss took fire and burned through her anxiety, leaving only the purest of truths.

She loved him, and for now that was enough.

Thirteen

"Are you expecting visitors?"

Chloe waved her polo stick in the direction of the driveway, and Isabelle turned in her saddle—gingerly, since she still didn't trust herself not to spook her horse with a clumsy movement—and caught a familiar silhouette gliding in and out of view between the trees. Tonight Cristo was flying to Russia, an unavoidable meeting, and for a moment she'd hoped he might have cut short today's business. But no, this was the town car not his Aston Martin.

"My sister," she told Chloe. How like Chessie to arrive a day early and without warning…although she rather fancied shocking Chessie with her brand-new skill. In jodhpurs and long boots borrowed from Chloe, she even looked the part. "Can we ride down and greet her?"

"Don't see why not." Turning her pony around, Chloe whistled her dog Otto to heel and led their sedate procession across the parkland toward the house. Isabelle's intrepid skill was yet to progress beyond a walk. "Keep a firm hand on your reins," Chloe called over her shoulder. "Dini has quite a fondness for the shrubbery."

Isabelle kept a firm hand on her reins and a firm eye on her pony in case appetite overwhelmed his calm nature. She paid no heed to the car or its occupant until Chloe said, "Your sister doesn't exactly travel light, does she?"

The driver added another piece to the mountain of matched luggage at the foot of the stairs, and Isabelle shook her head. "I don't think that's Chessie's." In fact she knew it wasn't, even before a stylishly attired stranger stepped from behind the car and into view.

From this distance she bore no physical resemblance to Cristo, and yet Isabelle instinctively knew that this was his mother.

"It's Vivi," Chloe confirmed. "I wonder what she's doing here?"

"Another wedding emergency, I imagine."

"Could be that." Chloe's eyes twinkled above a cheeky grin. "Or she's come to scope you."

"No," Isabelle said weakly. Then more strongly, "She has no reason to do that."

"You're the first girlfriend Cristo has ever brought here. I imagine that is reason enough."

As that message sunk in, Isabelle's heart skittered again. *The first girlfriend he'd brought here.* If Vivi knew—Vivi, who wanted him married to Madeleine—then that might explain her arrival. It certainly explained the sick pitch of Isabelle's stomach.

"Do you want to ride up and say hello?" Chloe asked.

"Good grief, no!"

And before she could laugh off that horrified response, the distinctive sound of a helicopter's approach had Otto barking and spinning in mad circles and Isabelle grabbing a better grip on Dini's reins. Chloe narrowed her gaze at the sky overhead before declaring, "The cavalry has arrived. You're saved!"

The cavalry was only one—but the right one, Isabelle reminded herself as she hurried from the stables to the helipad. With nerves threatening to chew holes right through her, she needed his reassurance as badly as her next breath. A quick word explaining that Vivi had called him home to discuss a wedding-planning issue. A smile, a kiss, an arm flung around her shoulder and an invitation to "Come meet my mother."

Any of the above would have worked, but then Isabelle saw him appear from beneath the whirling beat of the craft's rotors and straighten. She'd seen him in a suit and tie before—this past week she'd watched him dress from naked skin into full business attire on many a morning—but there was something in his bearing right now that pulled her up short. Shadowy wisps of foreboding fluttered through her, halting her headlong rush to intercept him.

Perhaps it was the dark aviator shades. Perhaps the flat set of his mouth, the tightness of his jaw. And perhaps it was the manner in which he'd arrived, sweeping in by helicopter in answer to his mother's summons. Whatever the cause, suddenly the stretch of lawn between them opened into a chasm of doubts. She'd spent a week in his company, she'd witnessed one sliver of his life and she'd allowed herself to believe she might fit. Standing there in her borrowed clothes, she felt like a fraud and a fool. The places she fit best were alongside Meredith in the kitchen and Chloe at the stables.

She would have turned tail and scarpered back to the stables if Meredith hadn't appeared from the back of the house, gesturing for her to come. Damn. In the mudroom she pulled off her boots and took stock of herself in Chloe's too-tight breeches and a no-longer-clean polo shirt. She wanted to run upstairs and change, but before she made the stairs the phone started to ring and she paused a moment too long. Meredith hurried through from the kitchen bearing a tea tray, and when she spotted Isabelle her relief was instant. "Will you take this through to the morning room for me, Isabelle? I'm expecting a call from Colin. This is likely him now."

What could she do?

Approaching the room, her feet grew heavy. The door stood ajar, and she could hear the two voices clearly. Vivi was bemoaning her morning's travel at melodramatic length. "My son owns half the private jets in this country," she sniffed, "and I am forced to fly commercial."

"No one forced you."

"You did, holing up down here with this Isabelle who I am hearing about from all quarters. Of course I needed to see what the fuss was all about."

"You are reading too much into this," Cristo said, his voice dismissively cool.

Apparently his mother could not be dismissed so easily because she went on, undeterred. "Madeleine tells me she works as a house cleaner. Is this true?"

"Yes," Isabelle said. "Quite true."

Years of practice came to the fore as she glided into the room and across the Aubusson rug to the tea table. The silence was perfect—not one rattle of cups, not a tinkle of spoons. She put down the tray with smooth efficiency and prepared to pour.

"Tea, Mrs…?" She left the query hanging, since she did not know Vivi's present name.

"Marais," the woman supplied, her smile warmer than Isabelle had expected. Up close she bore quite a likeness to her daughter, and like Amanda her eyes shone with undisguised interest as she took Isabelle in. "But you, Isabelle, shall call me Vivi as all my children do."

There was a beat of pause, an awkward moment. Isabelle did not know quite what to say. She'd been prepared for Vivi's coolness, hostility even, but this apparent amiability had thrown her.

"Speaking of children," Cristo interjected smoothly, but his eyes sparked with irritation as he moved to Isabelle's side and encouraged her to sit. "Where *is* your toyboy?"

"Patrizio has a showing," Vivi replied, seemingly unperturbed by her son's barb. "He will be following in a few days. I came early because I could not wait to meet your Isabelle."

Cristo said something low, foreign.

"Don't be rude," Vivi snapped.

"I learned my manners from you, Mother."

"Rubbish, we both know you have far better manners than I. Now—" she turned her attention to Isabelle "—I believe you are coming to the wedding? My son has not told me, but Amanda says this is so. We will need to rearrange the tables slightly, but this is not a problem."

"Amanda was kind to invite me, but I haven't decided if—"

"Why ever would you not?" Vivi interrupted. Then she looked from Isabelle to Cristo, her expression disingenuous. "Oh dear, have I put my shoe in it? When Amanda told me that Isabelle was your date for the Delahunty event and that you'd brought her to stay at your home, naturally I assumed this was more than an *amourette*…."

"What this is," Cristo said evenly, "is none of your business."

Vivi even managed to make her scoffing reply sound elegantly European.

"Aren't you needed in Sussex?" Cristo continued. "Surely the wedding preparations cannot run without your interference."

"Everything is ready," Vivi said, "according to that wedding planner who has not earned her overpriced fee. If she does create any more dilemmas, we shall manage them just as well from here. In the meantime, I am going to enjoy a few restful days with you and Isabelle. Now, the tea. Are you pouring, Isabelle?"

On the outside Cristo maintained an unaffected facade—over the years, he'd learned it was the only way to shake Vivi when she sunk her teeth into something. If she couldn't create a drama, she grew bored and moved on. Unfortunately she had latched on to his relationship with Isabelle today, of all days, and he did not have the luxury of wearing her down, nor could he delay his trip to Moscow.

He hated the necessity of leaving Isabelle, halving the time he had left with her before Saturday's wedding. If it were possible, he would take her with him, but the negotiations were delicate, the accommodations uncertain, and now there was Vivi. Ever since he received the message from his driver—too late to change the course of his mother's actions—he'd been quietly fuming. Mostly because he'd been so obsessed with getting Isabelle into his bed, he'd missed the obvious.

Of course Amanda and Madeleine and Lord knows who else would have told her about Isabelle. Why hadn't he anticipated her reaction? He did not bring casual girlfriends to Chisholm Park. He didn't take them to the polo or walk hand in hand with them through the village and French kiss them against the courtyard wall of the Maiden's Arms.

Now Vivi had met Isabelle and declared her approval. Taking the stairs two at a time, Cristo shuddered. He did not trust Vivi at the best of times; an acquiescent Vivi roused all his suspicions. He'd brought Isabelle to Chisholm Park to escape his family and their machinations. Now he would have to make other plans.

Isabelle had excused herself a little while back, saying she needed to change out of her riding clothes, and he found her just out of the shower and pulling on clean underwear. Brief. Lace. Dusky blue. The sight distracted him for a good long moment, until she shrugged into a clean blue shirt and started buttoning. If not for Vivi's arrival and the changed plans he needed to put into effect, he would have stalked across the room and started unbuttoning.

"I will have the car run you into London," he said. "You can spend the next few days at Wentworth Square."

She paused in her buttoning. Her expression was trickily composed, and he had no idea what she was thinking or feeling. "Because of Vivi?"

"What do you think?"

"I think you don't trust me to deal with your mother."

"I did not bring you here to deal with my family," Cristo said, "especially my mother, who will have you measured up for a wedding dress before I return."

Something shifted in her gaze, something he couldn't catch before she shook her head and laughed softly. "I'm pretty sure I can prevent your mother booking the church. You have nothing to worry about there. I am used to difficult clients and…"

"You are not the housekeeper," he said curtly.

"If you prefer me gone—" her gaze fixed on his, steady and searching for a long moment "—I can have my bag packed in five minutes."

Backed into a corner of his own making, Cristo had to let her stay. He was not happy. The edge remained until he'd unbuttoned her shirt and backed her against the dresser and used his fingers and mouth to bring her to a quick, shattering climax. And when he finally stripped away the lace and buried himself in her silken heat, he leaned forward and spoke with hot intensity against her ear. "This is why you are here and why you are staying. This—" he backed off slowly, enough that he could look into her eyes "—is why I will be doing everything in my power to finish this business swiftly. So you will be here in my bed when I return."

He had thought sex would settle his malcontent; that and putting the basis of their relationship into clear words. But Cristo's dissatisfaction escalated from the moment he left Chisholm Park. The caveman approach was not him, and it niggled that Isabelle had accepted his dictate without any response.

It niggled more when every attempt to call, to explain, to apologise failed.

In the morning she was out riding with Chloe; later she'd taken Vivi to lunch; and when his late-night call went unanswered, he could not settle without knowing she was all right. That neither his boorish tactics nor Vivi's demanding temperament had sent her running for the hills. He tried Crash, who knew nothing, except that Chessie was to remain with him for a few more days.

Stewing over his lack of foresight—not only regarding Vivi's guerrilla tactics; why hadn't he given Isabelle a mobile phone?—he paced and waited until Meredith returned his curt message. "There's no need to worry," she assured him. "Isabelle and Vivi are getting along famously. They've gone into London to meet with Amanda. Something to do with dress fittings."

That explanation did nothing to soothe Cristo's aggravation. He could just imagine Vivi railroading Isabelle into doing her bidding…and Isabelle allowing it. Jaw set tight, he punched the keys to Amanda's number. She answered sleepily, but when she recognised his voice and his cutting tone she immediately launched into a lengthy explanation.

"I suppose you're put out about the bridesmaid thing, but honestly I had no choice. I needed someone who would fit into the dress without major alterations. I was going to ask Madeleine, but I couldn't risk pairing her with Alejandro in the wedding party. You know what those two are like together," she said with an audible shudder. "But Isabelle is perfect."

Cristo swore softly. "As a replacement bridesmaid?"

"Harry's sister took a tumble from a horse. She's broken her collarbone and banged up her shoulder. Gia said she'll be fine by Saturday, that she'll do it with her arm in a sling, but her mother won't hear of it, and Vivi agrees. She suggested Isabelle as a replacement, and for once she has got it right!"

"Did Isabelle have any say in this?"

"She took some convincing," Amanda admitted. "She was talking about not coming to the wedding at all, and I rather gather that's because of you. Are you afraid she'll get ideas?"

"No," he said sharply, remembering with a flash of irritation how she'd coolly told him he had nothing to worry about on that score. "Isabelle is far too sensible for that."

"She is sensible, isn't she, and very capable. I suspect she is the queen of organization. I wish she'd been around to help me plan the wedding. She is going to speak to the caterers tomorrow, just to make sure everything's sorted. Oh, and she's arranged for Vivi to have a facial at Aylesbury while she's doing that, so she is also smart, your Isabelle. You should not let her get away!"

Cristo had spent the past week getting to know *his* Isabelle; he did not need his family's approval. Nor did he need her virtues spelled out, especially not in such a heavy-handed, she's-the-perfect-woman-for-you fashion. "I give you enough latitude in other areas," he told Amanda sternly, "but my love life is off-limits."

"Well, yes, but it concerns me that she says she is returning to Australia. Even though Bill and Gabrielle Thompson offered her a job."

Cristo went cold. He knew nothing of this job offer from a high-profile professional couple, nothing about any future decisions. During the past week, they'd skirted around that topic; he'd assumed she would wait until Francesca's plans were decided before looking ahead.

Yet she'd discussed this with his sister?

His antsiness snarled into more, and his tense silence was enough encouragement for Amanda to keep on talking. "I only know because we ran into them outside the Ritz tonight. Apparently Isabelle worked for them when they were in Australia last year, and they said to call them whenever she wanted a change of location. When they saw her here, they immediately made a firm offer, but she said she was going back to Australia."

"That's her home," Cristo said shortly, but as he ended the call he felt hollow. Cold. Impotent being so far away and unable to speak to Isabelle. Suddenly the Antovic contract didn't matter as much as being where he needed to be. Home. With Isabelle. Sheltering her from his ravenous family and convincing her to remain after the wedding.

Fourteen

Isabelle didn't remember agreeing to the bridesmaid gig, yet here she stood in a fairy-tale concoction of shimmering pink with lace and pearl embellishments. Apparently she and Georgina Harrington were a similar size and shape, and the gown was sent with accessories to Chisholm Park. By chauffeured limousine. The only transportation more fitting would have been a horse-drawn glass coach.

"I can give you a tad more room here," Vivi decided, tugging somewhere in the back where Isabelle couldn't see. Nor did she care; she was more interested in the concept of Vivi doing the work. So far she'd been very adept at making work and offering suggestions—Isabelle as bridesmaid, for example—but not so big on the doing.

"Do you sew?" she asked.

Vivi's perfectly made-up face appeared from beyond the gown's voluminous skirt. "Beautifully," she said with the trademark family confidence. "I did my apprenticeship on Savile Row. That is where I met my first two husbands."

Isabelle tried not to look too astonished, but failed dismally. "Not both at the same time, I hope."

Vivi laughed, then sat back on her heels. "If Alistair had been in the same room as Juan Verón I would not have noticed him, and that would have been an immense shame." Her eyes met Isabelle's in the mirror. "All the good in Cristo, that is from Alistair. He was a good, good man. Too good for me."

Afraid that everything she felt might show in her eyes, Isabelle let her gaze drop away in feigned contemplation of the gown's adjusted fit. Over the past days she'd grown adept at parrying Vivi's questions and avoiding the deeply personal, but now she was trapped in weighty folds of pearl-encrusted taffeta and by the new gravity in the woman's dark eyes. There was no escape.

"I am not all bad," Vivi continued, "but I have made some impulsive decisions that were not always in my family's best interests. My heart is in a rush and I am a selfish woman. When I left Juan, he did not want me to take a thing."

Isabelle knew she wasn't talking about fripperies. She knew but she had to ask.

"Not even your children?"

"I tried to take my sons, but Alejandro ran away. I had to make a choice, you see, to leave with one son or to take Cristo back to his father and leave with none. Cristo did not understand why he had to leave his home and his brother—he hated this ugly, grey country. But I hoped that this one time, my selfish heart made the right choice."

"Why are you telling me this?"

"I suspect that Cristo will not, and I want you to understand." From her seat on the floor, Vivi reached up and touched Isabelle's hand. "He is everything that you see and he is so much more, Isabelle, with so much love to give. Yet I fear that I have spoiled his view of love and marriage. He is a man and so he is stubborn. He is my son and so he is a cynic. If you love him, Isabelle, you need to know this. That is all."

After completing the alteration, Vivi and her copious luggage left for Sussex. Chisholm Park seemed cavernous and empty and as she awaited Chessie's arrival, Isabelle found herself with too much time for reflection. Too much time to chew over the implications of what she'd learned from Vivi…and to fill in the gaps.

Vivi hadn't mentioned the marriages after her first two, and how those upheavals in her household had affected Cristo. Every time Vivi followed her selfish heart to a new man, her child also had to follow. To a new home, a new country, into the care of strangers. How could he not equate falling in love with disruption and change and loss, all inextricably linked? Could a belief entrenched from such an early age be overturned, especially by a man with no need to change? He had so much that he loved already—his business, his home, his horses, his family—how could he possibly want for more?

And beneath the flickering doubt in Isabelle's heart, a new hurt burgeoned. He hadn't shared much of his life at all. Despite all the time they'd spent together, all the long walks and pillow conversations, she had only grazed the surface of his past.

Walking and thinking brought Isabelle to her bedroom, the one she'd taken the first night she arrived at Chisholm Park and where she'd eventually unpacked and stored her things. She'd only slept here the one night, but maintaining the pretence of her own room had been her safety net. She'd used it after Vivi's arrival, when she'd been spooked by the reminder of this family's wealth and position. When she'd needed a hole to scamper to. This is where Cristo had found her afterward, when he'd wanted to send her away and she'd resisted. When she'd chosen to block out the message he'd delivered so clearly in words and in action.

In two days her commitment to Cristo and his family would end. It was time to start thinking about her future. Time to call Miriam to confirm her next position, time to pack her bags. The fairy tale was over.

Cristo returned to find his home as he liked it—blessedly free of uninvited guests. On her way out the door, Meredith confirmed that his mother had departed after lunch. Isabelle was upstairs packing. "Happy to be home?" she asked.

"You have no idea."

With the remnants of shattered tension shooting through his blood, Cristo longed to bound up the stairs, but the power of that desire lent him restraint. Wanting this strongly did not sit comfortably, but he'd not examined the reasons. He would convince Isabelle to stay; that was all that mattered.

Packing meant the room she'd insisted on keeping, and that's where Cristo found her...or at least the signs of her presence. The plain black suitcase she'd brought from Australia sat open on the bed, several neat piles of clothes beside it. Something about that innocent sight sat wrong, and by the time he'd prowled around the bed and inspected the partially packed bag he knew why.

He picked up white cotton underwear he'd never seen before, fingering the soft fabric as he inspected the rest of the contents. Everything was plain, clean, serviceable. No lace bras or silk camisoles or sheer panties. He saw nothing of what he'd bought her from Nina, nothing that looked suitable for the wedding weekend.

Sensing her imminent arrival, his head came up as though tugged on strings of anticipation. She stopped on the threshold to the bathroom. Her deepwater eyes widened with surprise and a fleeting glimpse of pleasure. He hated how she shut that down. How she limited her smile to a tentative welcome.

"I wasn't expecting you until tomorrow," she said.

"Is that why you're packing?"

Her gaze slid away to the suitcase, and she shrugged slightly as she came into the room. "I was feeling a bit lost, actually, and I decided to get a start on. I wasn't sure what time we'd be leaving tomorrow."

"Unusual choices for a wedding," he said, running his hand across a stack of T-shirts.

"This is my own stuff."

"I can see that."

"For when I leave here."

A simple exchange, it should not have been incendiary. But her cool, calm manner as she picked up the panties he'd discarded and placed them back in the case acted like gasoline on the fire of Cristo's mood. "Tell me about that," he said, folding his arms across his chest and narrowing his gaze on her carefully composed face. "When are you leaving?"

"That depends on Chessie, but after the wedding. I spoke to Miriam today, and she has a job for me next weekend."

"What about the job with Bill and Gabrielle Thompson?"

Shock flared in her eyes. She blinked it away. "How did you know about…" She puffed out a breath. "Amanda. It doesn't matter. I'm not taking it."

"Why not?" he persisted, shifting his body to block her

attempt to turn away. "What if your sister stays in England to have her baby? Have you considered that possibility?"

"It's one possibility, but I can't make plans based on maybes. Nor can I risk my current job."

"As a housekeeper."

Isabelle's head came up. "What is that supposed to mean?" she asked sharply.

"I mean it's a job you can get anywhere, with any service or any number of private clients, as demonstrated by the Thompsons' offer."

Irritated and ridiculously hurt by his put-down of her job, Isabelle struggled to maintain her composure. This could decline into a clash of tempers too easily—she'd sensed him spoiling for a fight the instant she came out of the bathroom—and the recognition of her feelings and the continuing flutter of hope that he might yet return them had her on an emotional edge. She could not do verbal sparring right now. Not without the risk of revealing too much.

"I have a home in Melbourne," she said with admirable calm.

"You could have a home here."

Despite every good intention, her stomach clenched with longing. "Are you saying that you want me to stay?"

"Yes," he said staunchly. "I am."

"And do what?" *This was long term, not a weekend, not an extra week of a fairy-tale affair. This was real life, and she had to be sure; she had to nail down the details of that reality.* "If I took a job with the Thompsons, for example, I would be expected to live in and to travel with them. And when you or Vivi or Amanda came to one of their dinner parties, I would be greeting you at the door and serving your meal. Is that how—"

"No." His head came up a fraction, his nostrils flared and

his eyes flashed with primitive fire. "You won't be living in with these people, and I want you by my side at the table."

"What are you asking?" she managed, her voice husky and barely audible above the singing of joy in her ears.

"That you stay here with me."

Isabelle moistened her dry lips. "I have no money, no income…"

"You don't need any. I will give you whatever you need."

He took her by the shoulders, brought her close enough to feel the lure of his body heat, and the temptation to yield was ever so strong and wrong, so wrong. Sucking in a breath, Isabelle steeled her shoulders and her willpower. "You are asking me to stay as your mistress, all expenses paid." She saw the truth of that in his eyes, felt the dismay like a punch in her stomach. "What will I do all day while you're working and travelling? Do I go to the spa, make myself beautiful, wait for you to bring me home jewellery and more fancy clothes?"

"You enjoy the stables. You can help Chloe and continue your polo lessons."

"That's a holiday, Cristo, not a life."

For a long moment she held his gaze without wavering, absorbing the reflexive tightening of his grip and the hardening of his black-eyed glare. Then she turned abruptly within his hold, breaking his grip and allowing herself a brief respite as she fumbled blindly with her clothes. What a fool she was to have expected more.

"What are you angling for, Isabelle? A proposal?"

His voice was low, flat, but every hair on the back of her neck stood up. She should have denied it, shouldn't have taken so long to respond, and when it came her laughter sounded brittle and unconvincing. "Of course not. I've known you less than a month."

"Some women believe that is enough time. They mistake lust for love."

Isabelle's shoulders tightened. The injustice of that comparison snapped in her eyes and her voice as she turned back to face him. "Some women might, but I am not Vivi. I do know the difference, Cristo, and I do not expect a proposal from you."

"Not even a proposal that we continue our current arrangement? If you prefer, I can get you a place of your own."

"Thank you, but no. This was always temporary—a weekend, a week, until the wedding. I want to keep my job and a shred of pride," she said. "I cannot do that as a kept woman. Now, please, let me finish packing."

Everything inside Cristo screamed *no*. He wanted to bend her to his will, make her see reason, wipe the frosty control from her face, but what else could he offer? How could he make her stay? If she had faced him with defiance or counterdemands he would know how to argue, how to respond, but he did not know how to deal with such a simple, composed request.

Let me finish packing.

He turned away, took several steps before his gaze fastened on the contents beyond the open closet doors. The red gown she'd worn to the gala. A heather-grey jacket she'd worn the night they walked to the pub. The bright sundress he'd slipped hands and mouth beneath, the day they'd picnicked by the lake.

When he heard the quiet snap of her suitcase closing, Cristo saw red. "You have forgotten these." In six quick strides he'd snatched up all the hangers. He tossed them on the bed. Returned to open drawers, gathering underwear and shoes and bags, everything he had bought for her.

"Stop," she said, the single word wrenched from her throat with the first uncensored emotion he'd heard all afternoon.

Horrified, she watched him dump another bundle on the bed. "Stop it, I said!"

"All yours, Isabelle. Consider them perks of the job."

"They were my uniform, that's all. I don't need them anymore."

"Nor do I."

Now he was done, Cristo stood back from the evidence of his panicked petulance and wanted to kick himself. Isabelle turned away again, but not before he'd seen the shimmer of moisture in her eyes. *Dios,* he was a dolt. He'd acted like a child deprived of his favourite toy, but he would not see her cry. She started to pick up the mess of his doing, and his jaw set with a new resolve.

"Leave them," he said, and when she kept on tidying he forced her away from the clothes and the bed. Feeling her tense up beneath his hands, seeing the trapped look on her face as she slapped at his hands, was too much to bear. He pulled her tightly held body close against his and wrapped her in his arms. "Forgive me," he murmured against her ear. "You are right. I did not want to hear you say no. I wanted to find a way to make it yes, and I could see you walking away. I lost it."

That was all he could think to say, but against his shirt he felt her hot tears, and those he had to stop. He smoothed a hand over her back, bent to kiss her face, felt the gradual melting of her tension beneath his hands, and despite the complexities of emotion that rampaged through his body, he could not stop. His hands dipped lower, pulled her closer to his quickening heat, and the comfort of his caress changed tenor. There was no other way to show her how well they fit, no other way to communicate the depth of his feelings.

When he undressed her, she did not resist. When he took her down onto the floor amid the mess of discarded clothes, she went willingly. When he made love to her every part with slow, thorough intensity, she responded with the same cries of fulfillment—but there was a sadness in her eyes and an inevitability tapping at the edge of his consciousness.

What if this is the last time? What if you never again taste the sweetness of her mouth and her skin? What if you never again experience this wild, soaring connection?

No matter how many times he turned to her that night, no matter how many times and ways he showed her how well they fit, he still felt oddly unfulfilled.

"Stay," he breathed against her sweat-dampened skin late in the night, and Isabelle nestled against his body and listened to his promises. He would get her a cottage in the country. He would find her a job, her own business if she would prefer. And each promise of what he could buy her or what he could make happen with his wealth and position only deepened her conviction to leave.

There was only one gift that would change her mind, one that didn't cost a penny, the one she feared he would always hold back.

His love.

Fifteen

The wedding was everything Isabelle had expected and feared. A beautiful, wonderful, miserable, emotionally exhausting roller coaster before she even arrived at the church. She did her bridesmaid's turn down the aisle without drawing unnecessary attention to herself, particularly from the man standing at the groom's side. As predicted, Justin Harrington had missed the rehearsal, and this was her first glimpse of Chessie's one-night stand. Tall, his bearing stiff and aloof, taking no interest in the procession of bridesmaids. *Phew.*

One by one they took their places and then, over the first trumpet blares of the processional, she heard the creak of pews and rustle of rich fabrics as the guests turned to watch the bride's entrance. Isabelle glanced sideways past the line of extravagant pink frocks and caught Hugh drawing a deep breath, and beyond him the ice-cold expression of his brother. She'd heard nothing but good about the responsible, dutiful elder Harrington since he'd been revealed as the father of Chessie's baby, but now—a shiver tingled the length of her spine—he looked so cold. Quickly she shifted her focus back to Hugh, found his attention riveted and his face wreathed in pride and love and simmering excitement as his bride approached. The bottom dropped out of her stomach.

This is what she ached for—not the ring or the pretty dresses, not massed roses and glorious music, but the meaning behind today's ceremony and the look on Hugh's face that said it all.

Sudden tears choked her throat, but that was all right. It was a wedding. She could disguise them behind a smile of feigned happiness. Her peripheral vision filled with tear-blurred white, and blinking rapidly she turned enough to see Cristo handing his sister over to her new life. And as he stepped away, his gaze lifted and caught on Isabelle's—a brief capture, a heartbeat, an intense stab of longing, that only compounded her I-want-this-for-myself wretchedness.

She was such a fool, thinking she could get through this day without revealing the extent of her feelings. She should have run when she had a chance; now she was trapped by the occasion and her duty. If only there'd been somewhere in this ridiculous dress to stow her iPod, she could have blocked out the solemnity of the vows and the depth of meaning behind them.

But music would not have blocked out the huge smile that spread across Hugh's face when the minister pronounced them man and wife. Nothing could have blocked out his whoop of delight as he grabbed Amanda by the waist and swung her up and around in an open display of triumphant joy. Spontaneous applause broke out through the church, the mood so buoyantly infectious that even Isabelle laughed.

Then she was swept up in a joyous procession from the

church, formal photos, and an endless greeting line at the exceedingly grand Aylesbury Hall. She'd thought the reception might be easier, but she'd not counted on the unusual interest in her…and the story of how she'd met Cristo. Someone—Vivi, she presumed—had embellished the story with enough dramatic flair that every second woman she met sighed, "How romantic." Several asked if there would be another wedding soon, and Isabelle wanted to shout the truth: he has everything he wants—why on earth would he marry me?

At her side, taking this all in, was Alejandro Verón. Absurdly handsome and an outrageous flirt, he should have proved the perfect partner. But his touch created none of the zing of his brother's, and his interest in her affair with Cristo—apparently he'd not been taken in by Vivi's version—made her uncomfortable. His questions seemed to seek a reason for Cristo's interest, and in the end she told him straight. "No, we don't have a lot of common interests other than sex."

"You are a realist," he said with calming approval as he ushered her to the floor to join the bridal waltz. "I can see that you are not taken in by all this wedding bull."

Obviously she was a better actor than she'd thought; those childhood lessons had really paid off.

"This is good," Alejandro decided, taking her into his arms. "You will deal well with my brother."

Usually Cristo dealt well with the strictures of duty, especially when they pertained to his family. Today they'd kept him from Isabelle at a time when he needed her close, reminding her how well they fit together and attempting to regain the connection they'd forged last week. But they hadn't spoken more than ten words, and he seethed beneath the weight of his responsibilities as host. Even now, with the traditional aspects of the reception finished, he could not relax and enjoy the party he had paid for. Everyone wanted to congratulate him on the splendid event. All he wanted was to cut in on his brother, to hold Isabelle in his arms.

"She and Alejandro seem to have hit it off," Vivi commented. She'd not missed the reason for his distraction; his gaze had been following the other couple around the floor. "She has won us all, your Isabelle."

"She is going back to Australia."

His graceful mother missed a step, but recovered quickly. "Have you asked her to stay?"

"Yes," he said tersely. "I have offered her a home, a job, her own business. I have done everything but beg."

"Then perhaps it is time to go down on your knees."

She was not suggesting he beg, but the notion of matrimony as a relationship cure was laughable when it came from Vivi. Cristo could not laugh, not even with the cynicism reserved for her. For the length of this exchange he'd lost sight of Isabelle in the swirl of dancing couples, but now he found her again.

Dancing with Justin Harrington.

Luck had been on their side. Harrington's last-minute arrival for the wedding meant no time for introductions or to learn that the last-minute bridesmaid was Isabelle Browne. Now Christo manoeuvred close enough to see Isabelle's face. She needed rescuing, fast.

Vivi had no complaint when he cut in on the other couple. Slipping from one man to the other, she took Justin's hand and steered him away with smoothly practiced skill.

"Thank you," Isabelle said shakily. "That was very well done."

"Vivi has her moments."

She tried a smile, but it trembled at the edges and Cristo fastened his hold. "He knows?"

"Someone was talking, he heard my name. I had to tell him about Chessie."

Dios. "You told him she's pregnant?"

"Only that she's here, at Chisholm Park. The rest is not mine to tell."

Relieved, he tucked her closer beneath his chin and dipped to press his lips briefly against her cheek. A small kiss, but the contact he craved. The rest of this dance was his to enjoy.

All day Isabelle's emotions had been building, a giant weight pressed against a wall of tightly masked composure, and all it took was the butterfly touch of Cristo's lips to bring that wall tumbling down. The shudder started deep inside and moved through her in a rush of heartfelt longing.

"Are you all right?" he asked, his breath warm against her ear.

Isabelle shook her head slightly. She could have blamed Justin, the shock of that ambush, but she was tired of make-believe. Sick of hiding the truth of her feelings. And when he drew back—enough to lift her face, to look into her eyes—she could not lie. "You were partially right," she said quietly. She lifted her hand from his shoulder, brushed her fingertips along his jaw. "Some women do fall in love in less than a month."

His head came up reflexively, and her gaze fell away with her hand. She did not want to see the shock in his eyes.

"It's all right," she continued quickly. "You don't have to say anything. I just wanted you to know."

Now it was done, she couldn't slip back into the bittersweet dance. She needed space to breathe and compose herself, perhaps to lash herself for that burst of honesty, and when a couple dancing energetically by bumped into Cristo, she took advantage of their profuse apologies to tug her hand free of his and slip away.

The knowledge that he would follow and demand further explanation—possibly even use her vulnerability to change her mind—leant her feet desperate speed. She didn't know where she was going—she just needed solitude, and she headed out into the maze of gardens, kicked off the constrictive heels that hadn't fitted her properly and kept on running.

She didn't stop until walls of hedges halted her progress, and she sank onto a nearby garden bench. Winded, her breath rasped painfully in her lungs, and when she leaned forward to ease the pressure, the wetness of tears spilled from her face to mark the bodice of her frock. It was a shock to learn she was crying. It was a bigger shock to discover she was not alone.

"Trouble in paradise?"

She recognised the sneering edge to the voice without looking up. More than two hundred guests, and it had to be Madeleine. She didn't answer; there was nothing to say, but that didn't stop her tormentor. Isabelle heard the swish of her dress coming closer, and she tensed reflexively.

"If you're trying to escape, too, there's a gate down here."

That sounded surprisingly helpful, and when the dress swished on by, Isabelle caught the edge of agitation in the movement and looked up. Shoes in one hand, purse clutched in the other, Madeleine was stalking toward the far end of the garden room. Escaping, too?

When she stumbled unsteadily, car keys and shoes tumbled from her hand to the ground. Isabelle sat up straighter. "You're not driving…?"

"I don't intend walking all the way home."

Alarmed, Isabelle bit down on her irritation. "Since you can't walk straight, that would not be a good idea."

Hunkered down and still struggling to gather up her shoes, the other woman cut her a look. "Do you have a better one?"

A smile ghosted across Isabelle's lips as she remembered where Madeleine's home was located. *Oh, the irony of chance.* "Actually, I do." She rose on steady feet and held out her hand. "If you give me your car keys, I will drive you."

She'd gone. Cristo didn't know how or where to, but Isabelle had disappeared. At the wedding he found only her shoes, a pair of ridiculously high-heeled sandals discarded on the terrace steps. In the room they'd shared the night before the wedding, where he'd intended to woo her again tonight, he found the bridesmaid's dress and an insultingly brief note.

"Thank you for everything. Love, Isabelle."

It was enough to get his hackles up, to send him chasing back to Chisholm Park, but somehow she'd managed to outrun him. The suitcase packed with her own things was gone; the clothes from Nina's hung neatly in the closet. There was no second note—perhaps she thought everything had been said, but she was very much mistaken.

Wherever she had gone he would find her and he would have the right of reply. He didn't know if he could change her mind, if what he had to offer was enough to make up for his wrongheadedness when he'd returned from Russia—even if he was what she wanted.

But the thought of his life without Isabelle stretched before him, infinitely longer and more dismally grey than his first

English winter, and he knew that he would offer everything that he feared and more. To keep Isabelle in his life, he would offer whatever it took.

Isabelle could hardly believe her unexpected good fortune. Madeleine had proven a most worthy accomplice, not only in providing an escape from the wedding, but she'd then offered Isabelle the loan of her family's seaside cottage. "Why are you helping me?" Isabelle asked, suspicious.

"You're leaving Cristo," the other woman said. "Why wouldn't I help?"

She hadn't wanted to take up that offer, but in the end it was her only option. Justin Harrington had beaten her back to Chisholm Park, he'd spirited Chessie away to London and although her sister sounded confident of working out a solution, Isabelle remembered the man's haughty demeanour and she worried.

She couldn't leave England yet, not without knowing that Chessie's plans were solid and in *everyone's* best interests, not only that cool-eyed aristocrat's.

And as if to clinch the deal, she learned that the Delahuntys' cottage was in a quiet Cornish village, a stone's throw from the beach. Isabelle never felt more at home than walking on the beach and around the cliff tops. Every day she walked and she chewed over her options. If her sister stayed in England, she liked the idea of being close. Part of her growing family. She could get a housekeeping position, perhaps cook or butler, but she hated the thought of running across Cristo. Or even Vivi or Amanda or Madeleine.

When she grew tired of the incessant eddying of her thoughts, she plugged in her earphones and filled her head with music. That was today's choice. That's why she didn't hear the helicopter zooming in from the east or hovering above the cliff top in preparation for landing. That's why she had no warning at all until she reached the end of the beach, turned and there he was at the foot of the stairs leading up to the cottage. Even from this distance she knew it was him, by the set of his shoulders, the exact way he held his head, the loose roll of his limbs as he started toward her. And mostly by the crazy leap of her heart.

She stood stock-still in the sand as he cut down the space between them. She didn't consider running. She didn't even think to pull the buds from her ears and turn off the music. She heard nothing but the mad, out-of-control thunder in her heart.

He stopped in front of her, tall and unbearably attractive with the wind whipping the ends of his hair and plastering his shirt to his chest. Sunglasses hid his eyes and his expression gave away nothing. Not even the hint of a smile as he reached out one hand and removed the earphones.

"Thank you." A silly thing to say, but that's what came out. She cleared her throat. "How did you find me?"

"By the trail of shoes."

Isabelle frowned, not understanding, but then he reached behind him and pulled one of her flip-flops from his hip pocket. "Yours?"

Of course it was. She'd left them on the stairs. "I meant here, in Cornwall."

"That was considerably more difficult," he said with great solemnity.

"I'm sorry."

"Are you?" One corner of his mouth quirked. Almost a smile, but one edged in tension. "I rather thought that was the point."

Yes, of course it was, but he'd thrown her with his out-of-the-blue appearance. The *sorry* had just slipped out, an automatic response to being put on the spot. "I suppose Chessie told you I'd come here."

"Eventually. And only after extracting a promise."

"Oh?" As far as intelligent responses went, that ranked up there with *sorry,* but Isabelle was busily backpedalling, trying to recall what she'd told Chessie in their phone conversations. Trying to work out what kind of promise she might extract from him. And since he hadn't jumped in to tell her, she had to ask, "What have you promised?"

"That I won't break your heart."

Her heart had not settled down from its first thunderous leap, but now it took off at a frantic gallop of fear and hope and expectation. "How can you make such a promise?"

"Because I had to," he said with a hitch of one shoulder. "You ran away, Isabelle."

And he had to chase—he still could not accept no as an answer. She shook her head slowly. "You are not used to women running away, I'm sure."

"Not after they have told me they love me, no. That *is* what you were saying at the wedding?"

"You didn't have to make idle promises," she said in a rush, ignoring the directness of his question. "Chessie should have told you that I am sticking around a while, at least until she decides where she's having the baby. Then I will decide what I'm doing."

"She told me." He tipped the sunglasses to the top of his head, revealing eyes that burned with grim determination and something else she dared not attempt to identify. "I'm not here to make idle promises, Isabelle. I'm here to ask why you didn't give me the right of reply before you ran."

"I didn't want you to say something you didn't mean."

"I hope I am not a man who says things I do not mean, although this past week I have talked all the way around what I need to say to you, Isabelle. I have thought about my life without you and my life since I've met you." He lifted a hand to her face, mimicking the way she had touched him on the dance floor at the wedding. "Perhaps this colour you bring into my life is love."

"Perhaps?" she managed, a bare whisper of breath. A big beat of hope in her chest. "You are willing to risk breaking my heart for perhaps?"

"I will look after your heart, Isabelle, if you will look out for mine."

And when she looked into his eyes, she saw the vulnerability, and her own heart melted. "I do not fall in and out of love," she told him. "For me, this is it, once and forever, the only time I have ever felt this craziness. So please do not lead me on. Please do not offer anything unless you are certain that I am the one—not just because you want me now and not only for the weeks you spend at Chisholm Park where I do fit in, but for all the parts of your life where I do not fit."

"You fit me just fine, Isabelle Browne."

"In the country doing ordinary things, yes. At the stables, yes. In bed, yes."

His eyes glittered narrowly. "A point I would rather you didn't share with my brother in future."

Isabelle opened her mouth and shut it again.

"My family likes to talk and to interfere. They love to create drama. They're not good at leaving well enough alone, but in this instance they are right. You are the one for me, Isabelle. I cannot offer you the peaceful life that you prefer, but I can give you the home that you crave and I can offer you my heart."

To her amazement and soaring delight he went down on one knee in the sand. "You don't have to do this," she said. "Not unless you're sure."

"I am sure," he said, and the look in his eyes was everything Isabelle had ever wanted. "You are the colour in my life, Isabelle, the one I want to wake up beside every morning, to make love to every night. Will you be my wife, for better and for worse?"

"Yes," she breathed, sinking to her knees in front of him. His hands cupped her face, hers touched his lips and all she could feel was the better. "For ever after, yes, please."

* * * * *

Watch for Francesca and Justin's story, coming soon from Bronwyn Jameson and Silhouette Desire®.

The dark figures on the dock were still firing. The bullets cutting through the surface of the water without the warning boom of shots told Eve they were using silencers.

That was to her benefit. Silencers decreased the accuracy of every shot and lessened the range.

She grabbed for the rocks. Scrambled through the darkness. Bumped her knee on a boulder. Cursed.

Burrowing into the waist-deep grass, she kept low and crawled forward. Faster. Pushed harder. Needed as much distance as possible.

Shots pinged on the rocks.

J.T. scrambled alongside her.

He was breathing hard.

They had to stay close to the ground until they reached the next row of warehouses. Even though she was relatively certain they were out of range at this point, she wasn't taking any risks. And she wasn't slowing down.

J.T. had to keep up.

The splat of a bullet hitting the ground next to Eve had her rolling left. Maybe they weren't completely out of range.

She bumped J.T. He grunted.

His injured arm. Dammit. She could apologize later.

Half a dozen more yards.

Almost in the clear.

As she reached the cover of the alley between the first two warehouses she tensed.

Silence.

No pings or splats.

She glanced back at the dock. Deserted.

Time to run.

Her car was parked another block down.

Pushing to her feet, she sprinted forward. The wet bag dragged at her shoulder. She ignored it.

By the time she reached the lot where her car was parked, she had dug the keys from her pocket and hit the fob. Six seconds later she was behind the wheel. She hit the ignition as J.T. collapsed into the passenger seat. Tires squealed as she spun out of the slot.

"What the hell did you do to me?"

From the corner of her eye she watched him shake his head in an attempt to clear it.

He would be pissed when she told him about the tranquilizer.

She'd needed him cooperative until she formulated a plan. A drug-induced state of unconsciousness had been the fastest and most efficient method to ensure his continued solidarity.

"I can't really talk right now." Eve weaved into the right lane as the street widened to four lanes. What she needed was traffic. It was Saturday night—shouldn't be that difficult to find as soon as they were out of the old warehouse district.

A glance in the rearview mirror warned that their unwanted company had caught up.

Sensing her tension, J.T. turned to peer over his left shoulder. "I hope you have a plan B."

She shot him a look. "There's always plan G." Then she pulled the Glock out of her waistband.

Cutting the steering wheel left, she slid between two vehicles. Another veer to the right and she'd put several cars between hers and the enemy.

She was betting they wouldn't pull out the firepower in the open like this, but a girl could never be too sure when it came to an unknown enemy.

Deep blending was the way to go.

Two traffic lights ahead the marquis of a movie theater provided exactly the opportunity she was looking for.

The digital numbers on the dash indicated it was just past midnight. Perfect timing. The late movie would be purging its audience into the crowd of teenagers who liked hanging out in the parking lot.

She took a hard right onto the property that sported a twelve-screen theater, numerous fast-food hot spots and a chain superstore. Speeding across the lot, she selected a lane of parking slots. Pulling in as close to the theater entrance as possible, she shut off the engine and reached for her door.

"Let's go."

Thankfully he didn't argue.

Rounding the hood of her car, she shoved the Glock into her bag, then wrapped her arm around J.T.'s and merged into the crowd.

With her free hand she finger-combed her long hair. It was

soaked, as were her clothes. The kids she bumped into noticed, gave her death-ray glares.

They just didn't know.

As she and J.T. moved in closer to the building, she grabbed a baseball cap from an innocent bystander. The crowd made it easy. The kid who owned the cap had made it even easier by stuffing the cap bill-first into his waistband at the small of his back.

Pushing through the loitering crowd, she made her way to the side of the building next to the main entrance. She pushed J.T. against the wall and dropped her bag to the ground. Peeled off her T-shirt and let it fall.

His gaze instantly zeroed in on her breasts, where the cami she wore had glued to her skin like an extra layer. A zing of desire shot through her veins.

Not the time.

With a flick of her wrist she twisted her hair up and clamped the cap atop the blond mass.

"They're coming," J.T. muttered as he gazed at some point beyond her.

"Yeah, I know." She planted her palms against the wall on either side of him and leaned in. "Keep your eyes open. Let me know when they're inside."

Then she planted her lips on his.

* * * * *

Will J.T. and Eve be caught in the moment?
Or will Eve get the chance to reveal all of her secrets?
Find out in
THE BRIDE'S SECRETS
by Debra Webb
Available August 2009
from Harlequin Intrigue®.

You're invited to join our Tell Harlequin Reader Panel!

By joining our new reader panel you will:

• Receive Harlequin® books—they are FREE and yours to keep with no obligation to purchase anything!
• Participate in fun online surveys
• Exchange opinions and ideas with women just like you
• Have a say in our new book ideas and help us publish the best in women's fiction

In addition, you will have a chance to win great prizes and receive special gifts!
See Web site for details. Some conditions apply.
Space is limited.

To join, visit us at
www.TellHarlequin.com.

Tell
HARLEQUIN

REQUEST YOUR FREE BOOKS!

2 FREE NOVELS PLUS 2 FREE GIFTS!

Passionate, Powerful, Provocative!

YES! Please send me 2 FREE Silhouette Desire® novels and my 2 FREE gifts (gifts are worth about $10). After receiving them, if I don't wish to receive any more books, I can return the shipping statement marked "cancel". If I don't cancel, I will receive 6 brand-new novels every month and be billed just $4.05 per book in the U.S. or $4.74 per book in Canada. That's a savings of almost 15% off the cover price! It's quite a bargain! Shipping and handling is just 50¢ per book.* I understand that accepting the 2 free books and gifts places me under no obligation to buy anything. I can always return a shipment and cancel at any time. Even if I never buy another book, the two free books and gifts are mine to keep forever.

225 SDN EYMS 326 SDN EYM4

Name	(PLEASE PRINT)	
Address		Apt. #
City	State/Prov.	Zip/Postal Code

Signature (if under 18, a parent or guardian must sign)

Mail to the **Silhouette Reader Service:**
IN U.S.A.: P.O. Box 1867, Buffalo, NY 14240-1867
IN CANADA: P.O. Box 609, Fort Erie, Ontario L2A 5X3

Not valid to current subscribers of Silhouette Desire books.

Want to try two free books from another line?
Call 1-800-873-8635 or visit www.morefreebooks.com.

* Terms and prices subject to change without notice. Prices do not include applicable taxes. Sales tax applicable in N.Y. Canadian residents will be charged applicable provincial taxes and GST. Offer not valid in Quebec. This offer is limited to one order per household. All orders subject to approval. Credit or debit balances in a customer's account(s) may be offset by any other outstanding balance owed by or to the customer. Please allow 4 to 6 weeks for delivery. Offer available while quantities last.

Your Privacy: Silhouette Books is committed to protecting your privacy. Our Privacy Policy is available online at www.eHarlequin.com or upon request from the Reader Service. From time to time we make our lists of customers available to reputable third parties who may have a product or service of interest to you. If you would prefer we not share your name and address, please check here. ☐

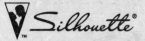

Silhouette Desire

COMING NEXT MONTH
Available August 11, 2009

#1957 BOSSMAN BILLIONAIRE—Kathie DeNosky
Man of the Month
The wealthy businessman needs an heir. His plan: hire his
attractive assistant as a surrogate mother. Her condition: marriage.

**#1958 ONE NIGHT WITH THE WEALTHY RANCHER—
Brenda Jackson**
Texas Cattleman's Club: Maverick County Millionaires
Unable to deny the lingering sparks with the woman he once
rescued, he's still determined to keep his distance…until her life is
once again in danger.

#1959 SHEIKH'S BETRAYAL—Alexandra Sellers
Sons of the Desert
Suspicious of his former lover's true motives, the sheikh sets out
to discover what brought her back to the desert. But soon it's
unclear who's seducing whom….

#1960 THE TYCOON'S SECRET AFFAIR—Maya Banks
The Anetakis Tycoons
A surprise pregnancy is not what this tycoon had in mind after one
blistering night of passion. Yet he insists on marrying his former
assistant…until a paternity test changes everything.

**#1961 BILLION-DOLLAR BABY BARGAIN—
Tessa Radley**
Billionaires and Babies
Suddenly co-guardians of an orphaned baby, they disliked each
other from the start. Until their marriage of convenience flares
with attraction impossible to deny….

#1962 THE MAGNATE'S BABY PROMISE—Paula Roe
This eligible bachelor must marry and produce an heir to keep
the family business. So when he discovers a one-night stand is
pregnant, nothing will get in his way of claiming the baby—and
the woman—as his own.

SDCNMBPA0709